The Trouble With Charles

The Trouble With Charles

By

Janet Cameron Simm

*Blackie & Co
Publishers Ltd*

A BLACKIE & CO
PUBLISHERS LIMITED PAPERBACK

© Copyright 2001
Janet Cameron Simm

First published in 2001

A CIP catalogue record for this title is
available from the British Library

ISBN 1 903138 12 4

Blackie & Co Publishers Ltd
107-111 Fleet Street
LONDON   EC4A 2AB

Cover Design by
Alexander Cameron Simm

Printed and Bound in Great Britain

DEDICATION

To Dr K H C Hester, my late father, for all his help and support.

ACKNOWLEDGEMENTS

My long-suffering husband, Alexander

My brother, Richard Hester, for his help regarding delinquent youth

The ladies of the Frome reference library

A kind gentleman at the AA for his help regarding driving with a disability

CONTENTS

CHAPTER ONE

Katrina woke early and, looking round, couldn't remember where she was at first. When her dozy brain eventually cranked into gear a smile spread across her face. Today was the first day of the rest of her life. The move was behind her and she had no one to think about but herself. It was a great feeling. She lay in bed watching the patterns on the ceiling that the sun was making through the branches of the old apple tree and marvelled at the changes that had taken place in her life over the past year. No more Peter, no more big house and garden, no more boring committees and big dinner parties. It was as if her life had gone into another phase and this time she was going to do it her way, though as yet she wasn't quite clear what her way was exactly.

Her first priority was to get her new little house in order. She had bought it from a little old man named Mr Pan who had had to sell and move into a home after the death of his wife. Katrina had felt almost guilty about buying the house and thus speeding his move. He had looked so sad and defeated, so she had promised to visit him when she could and give him a report on his beloved garden. She suspected that very little had been done in the way of decoration in the house for some years, but the garden was superb.

Half an hour later she was sitting at the big old kitchen table eating her breakfast and basking in the morning sun as it poured through the window. Outside, in the garden, the flower beds were a picture, mounds of colour fighting for space in the overcrowded earth. Mr Pan had done her proud and she certainly wouldn't have to do much work out there for a while.

The silence and her thoughts were shattered by the front door bell. It was probably Penny, who had said she would come round as soon as she had dropped off the boys at play school. She rushed to the front door, enthusiastic to show her daughter round her new property. To her surprise, instead of Penny on the doorstep she found a tall, dark, well built man of about her own age dressed in a smart dark suit and holding a large bunch of dahlias in his hand.

1

"Good morning," he said with a little bow, handing her the bunch. "My name is Charles Harris and I live next door. I saw you moving in yesterday and brought you these as a welcome present. I do feel that neighbours should be friends, don't you?"

Katrina was a little taken aback. Over the twenty years she had lived in her previous house she had hardly spoken to her neighbours, let alone been friends.

"Thank you, how kind," she said gaining her composure and taking the flowers. "They are beautiful. Will you come in and have a coffee? I have some freshly brewed."

"No thanks, I have to get to work. Another time perhaps." He turned and went down the path. Katrina gazed after him and hoped he remembered to call back. He was charming.

Penny arrived just in time to see him leaving. As she went into the house with her mother she asked, "Who was that gorgeous man?"

"That was my new neighbour. He brought me these flowers, wasn't that kind?"

"Certainly was. Wish I had neighbours like that."

"You can't have everything," scolded Katrina. "You have a perfectly gorgeous husband instead. Now, do you want some coffee before we start on my mess?"

"Thanks, that would be great," replied Penny, laughing at her mothers rebuke.

They went into the little kitchen and Katrina poured coffee and finished off her cold toast.

"How are you feeling this morning after the big move?" asked Penny as they drank from steaming mugs. "Any regrets now you are actually ensconced?"

"I was just thinking, I feel better this morning than I have for ages. At last I have my own space and can do exactly what I like with it. My plan is to paint all the downstairs rooms and get them nice first.

I also need new curtains and carpets. Luckily your father is paying me enough maintenance to allow me to do all these things without financial worry, as long as I don't get too rash. It should be fun."

"Rather you than me," her daughter replied. "I hate decorating, I leave it all to James."

"Well it takes all sorts," laughed Katrina. "When you're ready, shall we go upstairs and see what we can do with all the packing boxes up there first?"

Mother and daughter collected cleaning materials and went up to the bedrooms to spend a busy morning cleaning out cupboards and putting away clothes and linen, until it was time for Penny to collect her boys from play school.

"Thank you so much for all your hard work," said Katrina, kissing her daughter goodbye. "Give my love to the family, see you soon."

"I'll ring you Mum. Don't overdo the decorating and watch out for that neighbour of yours."

Katrina grinned and waved as her daughter drove off.

The next couple of weeks flew by for Katrina, in a flurry of cleaning and painting. She got a man in to measure up for carpets and curtains and all in all felt rather pleased with her efforts. At the end of the second week Penny phoned.

"Would you like to come over for Sunday lunch Mum? I'm sure you could do with a break."

"Thanks Penny, that would be great. As you say I could do with a change of scene. Shall I come about twelve?"

"Yes, fine. See you then."

Sunday dawned bright and sunny and Katrina looked forward to a day out with her family. Apart from the carpets and curtains that hadn't arrived yet, downstairs was finished and she felt the upstairs could wait for a bit. While she had been working her thoughts had turned to the problem of what she was going to do for the rest of her life. What she needed was a job of some kind. Next week, perhaps she would see what she could find.

She arrived at Penny's house at midday and was greeted on the doorstep by Max and Josh, her two young grandsons.

"Grandma, grandma, we've made you a special lunch and we are going to have it in the garden," cried Josh, taking her hand and leading her through the house into the garden.

Penny was in the garden putting the final touches to the big table that was placed in the shade of the beech tree at the side of the garden. She gave her Mother a hug.

"Lovely to see you Mum. Have a seat and I'll go and get some drinks and my wayward husband."

Katrina sat in the sun and talked to her grandsons about what they had been up to since last they met, until James and Penny joined them with a tray of drinks.

"Why don't you boys go and have a play on the climbing frame while daddy and I have a chat with grandma," suggested Penny hopefully.

"We want a chat too," insisted Josh.

"Very well then, but you will have to sit quietly," warned Penny.

The little boys sat on the grass with their orange juice for a while and then got bored and wandered off to play.

"How's the painting going?" asked James. "I hear you are going great guns."

"I've decided to give it a rest for a while," said Katrina, sipping at her cool white wine. "I have been considering the idea of getting myself a job."

"Really," exclaimed James in surprise. "I thought you were getting a good sum in maintenance from Peter."

"I am. It's just that I need something to do that will bring me into contact with other people. I want to meet people who know me as me, not as Peter's divorced wife. Can you understand that?"

"Yes, I see," answered James, looking pensive.

"Have you anything particular in mind?" asked Penny.

"No," replied her mother, trying to think of something she might aim for. "The trouble is I have no qualifications. I wish now I had learned to type or something. Perhaps I shall have to go back to school and learn a new skill. We'll see."

"Good luck I say," said James. "Maybe you should take up house design. Penny says you are making a wonderful job of the cottage."

"It's certainly a thought," agreed Katrina. "I don't think I would be brave enough to set something like that up by myself though. Having never earned a living before in my life I think I shall feel happier working for someone else first, until I get more confidence."

"You're probably right," said James. "You don't want to rush into something and find you can't cope."

At that moment Josh arrived and announced he was hungry and so was Max and could they have lunch now please? The adults laughed and taking the hint went in to get the food.

Lunch was delicious, fresh salmon salad with home made apple pie and cream to follow. It was the first proper meal Katrina had had since her move and she enjoyed it even more than usual. When everything was cleared away they all decided to walk in the park and feed the ducks.

The park was quite full that afternoon, with people walking off their Sunday lunches. Katrina could remember walking here with Penny and Mark when they were small. Now here she was with her grandchildren. Josh and Max fed the ducks and then they all walked round the lake and back towards the car. As they wandered Josh took Katrina's hand.

"Mummy says we have to look after you because you are sad. You don't look very sad. Are you better now?" enquired the little boy.

'Out of the mouths of babes' thought Katrina, wondering how to answer his question.

"You are right, today I am very happy spending the day with you, but sometimes I do get a bit sad. Thank you for looking after me."

"Why are you sad?"

"Because grandpa Peter is now living with Shirley and sometimes I get lonely all by myself."

"Oh I see," said Josh apparently satisfied with her explanation and, deciding that his grandma didn't need him for the moment, he dropped her hand and went off to play with his brother.

"Sorry about that," said Penny looking rather embarrassed.

"Don't worry. It must be confusing for them, all this divorce nonsense. It's sweet of Josh to care."

"As long as he hasn't upset you. I do try and explain it to them but it's very difficult."

"I'm sure," agreed Katrina putting her arm around her daughter. "I see the boys and James have got back to the car, let's run and join them shall we?"

Mother and daughter raced across the grass to the waiting car as the boys stood and cheered them on.

The following morning Katrina got up early and dressed carefully. She wanted to make a good impression if she managed to get any interviews. She parked the car and walked to the job centre. She had never been there before and as she walked in she began to feel nervous. It was a big office with boards all round the walls, where the job notices were pinned. On one side there were three large desks. Katrina stood and watched to see what everyone else was doing. People were taking cards from the boards and going up to the desks with them. She started studying the boards. She could find nothing that she could do, apart from cleaning offices or serving fast food. She was not that desperate.

After half an hour of searching she gave up and left. This was not going to be as easy as she had hoped. Perhaps she would have to take some sort of course after all. She walked dejectedly back towards the car. Suddenly a bright card in a shop window caught her eye. Could this be advertising a job? With fingers crossed she bent down and read the card.

WANTED PART TIME SALES ASSISTANT. APPLY WITHIN.

'Nothing ventured, nothing gained,' she said to herself and walked in. The shop was not large, but seemed well stocked, with bright clothes hanging on racks round the walls. At a large desk, to the right of the door, sat a smartly dressed woman, in her early thirties, Katrina guessed, working in a large ledger. She looked up as Katrina entered the shop.

"Can I help you?" she asked, "or do you just want to browse?"

"Actually I came in to ask about the job advertised in your window," Katrina replied. "Is it still available?"

6

"Yes. Have you had any experience of working in a shop?" asked the woman, looking Katrina up and down as she spoke. Katrina was glad that she had worn her best silk suit. After a second or two of toying with the idea of pretending she had worked in shops all her life, she decided to be honest and put her cards on the table.

"To tell the truth I have had no experience whatsoever, however I am usually a quick learner and am willing to work hard. Perhaps you could give me a trial."

The woman at the desk laughed. "You are certainly honest and that's a good start. I was really looking for someone who knew something about the job but never mind, I probably couldn't pay them enough anyway. I'll tell you what, let's say we see how we go for a month. After that if either of us are unhappy about the arrangement we can call it a day. How about that?"

Katrina was thrilled. She had a terrible urge to give this woman a hug, but managed to restrain her self. As calmly as she could she said, "That seems fair. Thank you very much. Could you tell me a few details about the job please?"

"Yes, of course. I should like you to work Mondays, Fridays and Saturdays from 9 till 5. £90 a week. No paid holidays. Work would entail serving in the shop, unpacking and putting out new stock, a bit of cleaning, making coffee. That about covers it I think. Basically I need someone to help run things so that I can get on with paper work and ordering and that sort of thing. What do you think? Would you be willing to do fairly menial work?"

"Sounds fine to me. When would you like me to start?"

"Next Monday suit?"

"Yes fine. I shall look forward to it."

Katrina left the shop feeling on top of the world. She had a job, even if it was only as a general dogs body. At least it was a start. She suddenly realised she didn't even know the name of her new employer. She turned and looked back at the little shop to see what it was called. "Susannah's" she read on the board above the beautifully arranged display window. Well maybe that was the answer.

That evening Penny phoned her.

"Well, how did it go?" she asked, ready with condolences in case her mother had been unlucky in her search.

"Seems I am employable after all," laughed Katrina proudly. "A very kind lady, who owns a dress shop in town has given me a job. Isn't it great? I start on Monday."

"Mum, that's wonderful. Congratulations. I do hope you enjoy it. Do you think you can cope with the temptation of working with all those clothes? I know your penchant for buying new outfits."

"I shall just have to be firm with myself. I don't think it is going to be easy though. The clothes are gorgeous."

"I can see all your wages being spent as soon as you get them," laughed her daughter. "Where is this shop by the way?"

Katrina explained. Penny promised to send all her friends round to buy new clothes.

The following day Katrina decided to go and visit Mr Pan in his nursing home, and see how he was getting on. She phoned and asked if it would be convenient for her to go about tea time and was told by the nurse that that would be fine, she would tell Mr Pan to expect her. That afternoon she drove to the nursing home and parked her car. It was a rambling building, probably several houses knocked into one, she supposed. She went through the front door and found herself in a big hallway, painted in pastel colours, with pleasing prints of old masters round the walls. On her right was a small office so she went across to ask her way. She was greeted by a cheerful young nurse who took her to find Mr Pan.

"He was really upset when he first came here," she explained to Katrina, "but he is beginning to cheer up a bit now. He's made friends with another old man and the two of them chat away all day, mostly about gardening I think."

"I moved into his old house, you know," explained Katrina. "The garden is quite beautiful. Could I take him out to see it one day do you think?"

"I'm sure he would love that," enthused the nurse. "Well, here we are at the common room. Mr Pan is over there by the window. I'll leave you to it."

Katrina walked over to the window. Mr Pan was sitting alone and staring out at the garden, but he looked up as she approached and beamed. Katrina was amazed at the change in him.

He had quite lost that defeated look that he had had when she first saw him.

"Hallo, Mrs Blackwell," he greeted her as she reached him. "You looking after my garden?"

"Doing my best," she replied laughing. "You look happy. They must be treating you well."

"Can't grumble. Three good meals a day. I miss my garden though."

"Maybe we could arrange for you to come with me and see it sometime. What do you think?"

The old mans face lit up. Katrina felt happy that she could give him such pleasure, so easily.

She left the nursing home three hours later, very pleased that she had made the effort to go, but relieved to be in the fresh air again after the rather stuffy atmosphere of the home. She had been introduced to several of the other "inmates" and had enjoyed chatting to them all and hearing their stories. It appeared to be a very well run establishment and she was happy that Mr Pan had settled so well. She could stop worrying about buying his house now.

A couple of nights later, as she was clearing up after her supper, the doorbell rang. Probably someone collecting for charity, she thought as she grabbed her purse on the way to the door. She was very surprised to find Charles Harris standing there on the doorstep looking casual, in slacks and open neck shirt, but just as handsome.

"Hope this is not too late for a call," he said searching her surprised face. "Thought I would come and claim that cup of coffee you offered the other day. Do say if it is inconvenient."

She smiled broadly and replied quickly, "Of course not. Come in. I thought you were collecting for charity."

Charles grinned and followed her into the sitting room. He looked round.

"My goodness, you've done wonders with this room. I used to come and visit the old couple here, now and again, and I seem to remember a lot of rather dirty cream paint everywhere. This pale green really makes this room look bigger."

9

"Glad you like it. I must say I am rather pleased with it and it will be even better tomorrow when the carpets arrive. Come through to the kitchen and I'll make that coffee."

Charles inspected the kitchen and decided he liked that too. Katrina had painted the walls a very pale yellow and all the woodwork grey with white trim. She had seen the colour scheme in a brochure and had immediately decided to copy it. They took the newly made coffee into the sitting room and sat down on Katrina's big easy chairs.

"Well, this is very pleasant," said Charles , leaning back in his chair.

The thought suddenly struck Katrina that she knew nothing about this man, yet she had blithely invited him into her house without a qualm. He could be a mass murderer for all she knew. She glanced at him sitting there, relaxed and elegant, sipping his coffee and decided he looked too good to be bad. It was too late to bother now anyway.

"Thank you again for those dahlias by the way," she said, feeling a need to start a conversation. "They lasted ages and were much admired by various visitors. Did you grow them yourself?"

"Yes, I find a bit of digging very relaxing after a hard day at work, and the blooms are so beautiful. All very rewarding. Your garden is looking very colourful. Do you enjoy gardening?"

"Not a lot, really, but Mr Pan has left everything in such good order there's not too much to be done. Just a bit of weeding now and again, and the lawn mowing of course."

"Well if you need any help any time, don't hesitate to ask. You know where I am."

"Thank you. I may hold you to that."

"Have you moved far?"

"No only from the other side of town. My daughter lives quite close so I wanted to stay in the area but needed something smaller."

"Ah I see. It is a nice part of the country isn't it?"

Katrina was pleased that he didn't ask why she needed a smaller house. She wasn't ready to tell this handsome guest about the divorce and all her troubles yet. They chatted on pleasurably

10

about the area and the convenience of being so close to London, until finally Charles decided it was time he went home before he outstayed his welcome. As he reached the door he turned, "Thank you for a lovely evening," he beamed.

"We must do it again sometime." Katrina found herself staring after him and hoping it wouldn't be too long.

On Monday morning Katrina got up early. She had not slept very well, worrying about the next day and the new job. By the time she reached the shop, just before nine, she was seriously wondering if she had done the right thing. She had a strong urge to run. As she stood on the doorstep, poised for flight, the door opened and her new boss stood smiling a welcome. It was too late.

"Good morning. Come in, nice to see you again."

"Good morning," Katrina replied stepping inside. 'Well here I go,' she thought, and took a deep breath as she followed her new boss to the back of the shop.

As she hung her coat up on a peg on the wall, Katrina looked round. The room was mainly a store, with boxes piled in one corner, several racks of clothes, a table in one corner with a kettle on it and two chairs. Susannah turned to Katrina and said,

"Welcome to the emporium. This is the storeroom as you can see. Shall we have some coffee before we start?" She went across to the kettle and filled it from the tap in the small sink. "My name is Susannah," she continued, "but call me Sue. I forgot to ask your name the other day."

"I'm Katrina. How do you do?"

"Nice name. Well, Katrina, your task for the morning is to get these clothes ready to go into the shop. Have you ever used a steamer before?"

"No I havn't actually. Could you show me?"

When they had finished their coffee Sue showed Katrina the steaming machine and how it worked. It looked simple enough. "If you have any problems just come and ask," continued Sue. "I shall be in the shop sorting out the dreaded VAT. O.K.?"

"Yes, fine," replied Katrina, with more confidence than she felt. By the end of the morning she had broken several fingernails getting the clothes out of their plastic covers, and her back ached

11

from bending down with the steamer. However the job was done and she felt rather pleased with herself. Sue gave her a half an hour lunch break and with a certain amount of relief she stepped into the sun and walked to the shops to find herself a sandwich.

As she sat munching her lunch, soaking up the sun, she felt utterly content with the world. She had her new house, her new job and her life was looking good at last.

The afternoon was a lot more enjoyable. Sue suggested that she should look through the stock and try and remember some of the prices, so that she could help customers find what they wanted. Several browsers came in and wandered round but no one seemed to want any help. Then just as Sue was thinking of shutting up shop in walked a smart little lady of about 70 wanting a new suit.

"I am going to Australia to see my son and his family," she explained to Katrina. "I need something to travel in that won't crush too much. Can you help?"

Katrina spent a very enjoyable half an hour helping the little lady find what she wanted and hearing her life history into the bargain. When she left at last, thrilled with her new purchases, Sue turned to Katrina and said, "You're rather good at this selling. Sure you havn't done any before?"

"No, honestly. I do enjoy it though I must say."

"Don't get too blasé," warned Sue. "It's not always that easy. Anyway I'm glad you enjoyed yourself. Let's go now. I'll clear these clothes up in the morning. See you on Friday."

Katrina drove herself home and had a long hot bath. She had not felt so happy for a long time. She had had a lovely day and felt that the job was going to be all right after all. The aches in her shoulders began to ease and she felt at peace with the world.

On Wednesday Penny came round to see how she was, after dropping the boys off at play school on the way. As they sat in the sitting room with their coffee she asked,"Well, how did it go? Do you think you will enjoy the job?"

"Oh yes. I spent all morning steaming clothes but in the afternoon I actually sold an outfit. Sue says I seem to have a natural ability to sell things, though to tell the truth it wasn't difficult. Sue seems to be a very nice person, though we didn't talk much. She was doing paper work most of the time."

"You will be going back on Friday then?" said Penny, grinning.

"You bet," replied her mother. "Can't wait actually. Hopefully we shall be busier on Friday and I shall have more to do. By the way, the gorgeous Charles came round again for a chat and a coffee. When he had gone I suddenly realised that I still don't know anything about him, what he does for a living and so on. He has promised to come again so I shall ply him with questions next time."

"You do that Mum, he certainly looked worth getting to know, a real dish," enthused Penny. "He's probably 'something in the city' I should guess, though maybe he looks a bit too fit for that, no paunch from all those business lunches." She thought a moment and then exclaimed, "He's probably a policeman."

"I don't know about that but he is certainly away a lot. Perhaps he is in some sort of sales job, travelling round the country selling things."

"I don't think so somehow," replied Penny thoughtfully. "He doesn't look the type somehow."

"No, true," agreed Katrina. "Anyway he seems very charming and that's the main thing. Offered to come and help with the garden which I thought was very kind."

"Always useful to have help on hand if you need it. Mind you if he is away such a lot he's not going to be too much help is he?"

Katrina nodded in agreement and then started on another tack.

"Have you seen anything of your father lately?" she asked tentatively.

Penny thought carefully before answering. Her mother obviously wanted to hear that her father was having a bad time with his new wife but in truth he seemed extremely happy. If Penny said that it would probably upset her mother for the rest of the day, so she answered vaguely, "Yes, he came over last week actually, to see the boys and so on."

Katrina realised that Penny was being tactful, and didn't press the subject further. They talked for a while about the boys, then Penny said it was time she went and got some shopping before she collected them again.

"Thanks for the coffee, Mum," she said kissing her mother goodbye.

Katrina waved her daughter off and returned to her housework. As she scrubbed out the bath, she began wondering whether three days work a week was going to be enough to occupy her. Now that she was on her own there was very little to be done in the house. It was not like the old days when Peter and the children were around to make things untidy. She suddenly felt very alone and deep down sad. She sat on the loo and sobbed. Would she ever come to terms with this awful loneliness, she wondered, as she let the tears stream down her face unchecked. Most of the time she was fine, then suddenly it would hit her like a great black cloud, enveloping her and obscuring everything but her misery. As yet she had found no antidote for it.

At last Friday came and she set off for work, glad of a purpose for getting out of bed.

"Morning, Katrina," said Sue letting her into the shop. "I've made you some coffee. When you have had it perhaps you could do a quick dust round, duster in the drawer over there."

Katrina drank her coffee and set to with the duster. By the time she had finished, the shop had several customers and she was able to go back to the much more pleasant job of selling clothes. Luckily she got the hang of the till quickly and also how to deal with credit cards. It was all so new. By the end of the morning she was quite tired. Her midday break was very short but she did manage to eat the sandwiches she had bought with her. By the time Sue locked up for the night they were both exhausted, but pleased with their days work.

Katrina did a bit of shopping on her way home and met several people she knew in the supermarket. They all asked what she was up to and promised to come into the shop when they heard where she was working.

Saturday was another busy day. Some people just came in to browse but there were still a lot of sales. Everyone remarked on how beautiful the clothes were and Katrina felt quite proud to be selling them, in spite of the fact that it was Sue who had chosen them all. She obviously had a very good eye.

That evening as Sue was locking up she thanked Katrina for all her hard work.

"I think we shall make a good team," she said. "I believe you rather enjoy selling clothes."

"Oh I do," said Katrina enthusiastically. "This job is just what I needed."

"Good. See you on Monday then."

Katrina felt she had been given a gold star by the headmistress!

Next day her son Mark phoned. They exchanged news then Mark said, "Would it be all right if I came over to stay next week sometime? I've got a week's holiday and would like to bring Sarah over to meet you. Would that be OK?"

"Yes, of course. I have to work on Monday but I'm at home Tuesday till Friday. You can stay on when I'm at work if you want to but I would rather I was there when you arrived."

"Of course Mum. We'll come about midday on Tuesday, if that's all right."

"Fine, I'll see you then. Is Sarah a vegetarian, by the way?"

Mark laughed on the other end of the phone. "No Mum. She eats anything within reason."

Katrina had a terrible urge to say what a change that was from his usual girlfriends, but thought better of it. Instead she said, "Look forward to seeing you both on Tuesday then. Bye."

Katrina put the phone down and sat wondering about Sarah. Mark had mentioned a new girlfriend at Christmas but was Sarah the same one? If so the relationship was lasting well. Mark usually changed girlfriends much quicker than that. Perhaps this time it was serious. Like most mothers, Katrina liked the idea of her children being married and settled, or at least settled, with a steady partner. After all Mark was twenty-five now and she had had two children by that age.

On Monday Sue and Katrina rearranged the stock. After the busy Friday and Saturday it was looking a bit depleted. They rearranged the clothes still left on the racks and brought more in from the stock room. Then Sue took everything out of the window and created a new display.

"There is nothing like a good shop window to bring in the punters," she said, standing back to admire her handiwork.

Later, as they were having a coffee break, Katrina asked Sue,
"Have you had a shop before?" She longed to know where Sue had come from and what her life was like away from the shop.

"No, not on my own at least. I used to be in partnership with a friend but it didn't work out, so we sold up, and I came here about six months ago. My aunt left me some money so I was able to put down a deposit on the shop. I feel much happier being in control, though the money side is a bit daunting sometimes. By the way, would you consider doing a few more hours from time to time? It's just that I would like to get out and get some more stock as time goes by. Of course, I wouldn't leave you until you are more settled. It's just a thought. I'd rather keep the shop open if I could."

Katrina was thrilled. Sue seemed to have great faith in her ability.

"Thank you for your confidence in me. I should be quite happy to do extra hours. I live alone with no one to look after but myself so there would be no problem."

"Great. That's settled then. I am so pleased you applied for this job, you are learning things fast and charming the customers into buying clothes. A great asset. Thank you."

"Thank you for being such a nice boss."

Sue grinned, "Now don't let all this go to your head," she scolded. "Come on there's work to be done."

Katrina laughed, "Slave driver," she responded and fled back into the shop, hoping she had not overstepped the mark.

Next day Katrina worked hard getting everything ready for Marks arrival. At midday his little green MG parked in the driveway. Katrina heard it and rushed to the front door to welcome her guests.

Mark ran to her and gave her a big hug then turning he took Sarah by the arm and drew her across to introduce her to his mother. She was beautiful, tall and slim with blonde hair falling round her shoulders. She smiled sweetly and shook Katrina's hand as Mark said, "This is Sarah, Mother."

"How do you do Mrs Blackwell. So nice to meet you at last."

"How do you do Sarah. Do call me Katrina. Now lets go into the house and I'll get the lunch under way. Would you like some coffee after your journey?"

"Yes please Mum, that would be great." They all trooped into the house and drank their coffee in the kitchen and chatted as Katrina busied herself with the lunch.

Later, when the meal was over they decided a walk round the park would be a good idea. It was a lovely day but too chilly to just sit in the garden and Mark felt that his lungs needed some fresh air after London.

"Are you a country girl?" Katrina asked Sarah as they walked along between the overflowing beds of flowers.

"Yes, I suppose I am. I was born and brought up in Hertfordshire. My sister and I had ponies when we were young and we used to ride for miles across fields and commons. Now, when I go home to see my parents, it seems to be all built up or made into golf courses. Sad really."

"We are lucky here to have two big parks. You couldn't ride in this one but the one across town has good bridle paths running through it. It's right next to where Mark's sister Penny lives. Great for the children. By the way Mark, speaking of Penny, I was thinking of inviting her and James to supper tomorrow. Would that suit you, or have you other plans?"

"That sounds great Mum. I'll give Dad a ring later and see if we can go over there on Thursday evening. I haven't seen him for ages and I feel I should make the effort now and again."

Katrina felt a horrible sinking feeling in the pit of her stomach. She hated her children going to see their father. It was so stupid but she couldn't help it. She tried desperately not to let her feelings show on her face and said cheerfully, "Fine. I'll wait till you have phoned your father before I phone Penny then. Now how about turning for home, I could do with a cuppa."

Later that evening Mark went off to phone his father and Katrina was left to chat with Sarah.

"You don't like Mark seeing his father do you?" asked Sarah, studying Katrina's face.

Katrina was taken aback with her directness. "You're right. And I thought I had made such a good job of hiding my feelings."

"Oh I don't think Mark noticed. I just happened to see your face when he announced that he was going to see his father."

"It's a quite unreasonable feeling and I do try and hide it but I just can't get rid of it."

"When you find yourself a new man you will probably feel a lot better I expect. At the moment you feel that the children are the only thing you have left from the marriage and you are scared that Peter is trying to poach them too."

"I like the way you say 'When I find a new man.' Chance would be a fine thing."

They laughed together and talked about less personal things until Mark joined them again after his phone call.

"It's all arranged then," he announced. " Penny and James tomorrow and father on Thursday."

Katrina went off and phoned Penny. Luckily she and James were free on Wednesday.

Next morning Mark and Sarah got up late. When they eventually surfaced about noon they had a brunch rather than breakfast.

"Oh what bliss," said Mark, tucking in to his fry up. "This is the life, getting up at midday and having a cooked breakfast."

"Well, I'm sure you have earned it. Now what are your plans for the day?"

"I thought I would take Sarah out for a drive, show her the countryside, if that's OK."

"Of course. I'll be busy here with the meal for tonight. Penny and James are coming over about 7.30 so don't be too late back will you?"

"Don't worry Mum. We'll be clean and tidy and ready to receive the guests by 7.15."

Mark was as good as his word and the little MG roared up the driveway again at 6. They had had a wonderful afternoon driving round with the hood of the car down and they looked windswept and happy.

"Do you want a drink or would you rather change first?" asked Katrina.

"Can we have a bath and change first? Is there plenty of hot water?"

"Yes, help yourselves. I'll open the wine ready for you when you come down."

"Thanks Mum." They disappeared upstairs and Katrina put the finishing touches to her table.

James and Penny arrived late with apologies and tales of babysitters who had no sense of time. It was a most successful evening. Katrina loved having her children all together and Sarah, as the newcomer to the party, fitted in perfectly. As Penny helped her mother stack dirty dishes in the kitchen after the main course she whispered, "Mark has certainly done well for himself this time. Isn't Sarah gorgeous?"

"She certainly is. When I think of some of the strange girls he has brought home, his taste is certainly improving."

They laughed and picked up the plates and the pavlova and went back to the dinning room to join the others. By midnight Penny was beginning to look very tired and she and James decided it was time they went home.

"Thanks for a lovely evening Mum," said Penny kissing her Mother.

"You're very welcome," replied Katrina opening the front door for her guests. "See you again soon. I'll give you a ring. Bye, James. Drive carefully."

She waved them off and went back into the house.

"Do you want a hand to clear up Mum?" asked Mark unenthusiastically.

"No thanks love, I'll do it in the morning. What are your plans for tomorrow by the way?"

19

"We thought we might go to the Arts and Craft show we saw advertised. Do you want to come too?"

"I'll see in the morning. I think I shall go up now, I feel a bit whacked."

"I'm not surprised," commented Sarah." That was a superb meal you made. Thank you so much for a lovely evening. I did enjoy myself. James and Penny are very good company, aren't they?"

"Well I must say I am very fond of them, but then I am biased. Good night you two. See you in the morning."

Next day, after another late breakfast, they all went off to the Arts and Craft show. It was held in the big church hall and was very well attended. They wandered round the tables studying the beautiful exhibits made of wood, pottery and glass, but carefully avoiding the stalls covered in kitsch pillows and ghastly home made dolls. Katrina was particularly taken with a beautiful wooden bowl made of pale wood that was big enough to take fruit. She could just see it on her kitchen table full of apples, oranges and bananas.

She was just studying the price when she felt a tap on her shoulder. Turning she found herself face to face with Charles Harris.

"Good gracious," she exclaimed. "Fancy seeing you here." She felt herself blushing and was very cross with herself.

"What a nice surprise. Are you going to buy that?" asked Charles grinning broadly as she clutched the bowl to her chest and looked embarrassed.

"I think I will," she said decisively and started getting out her cheque book. When she had paid up and had her bowl wrapped she turned back to Charles.

"Are you buying today or just looking?"

"I have only just arrived actually. I'm not looking for anything special but just dropped in to see what there was. I'm glad I did, there are some beautiful things here. I've also been meaning to come and see you to ask you out to supper with me on Saturday. You've saved me the trip. Can you come?"

"I'd love to, thank you," she said, hardly pausing before replying and then fearing she had seemed too eager and blushing again. "I'll pick you up at 7.30 then, OK?" said Charles, amused at her embarrassment.

"Fine. I shall look forward to it."

Just then Mark and Sarah arrived on the scene wanting Katrina's advice on a piece of glass Mark was thinking of buying. Katrina introduced everyone.

"Would you like to give your opinion on the glass Charles or shall we leave you to browse?" asked Katrina, not wanting to be rude to Charles by just walking off with Mark.

"No, you go. I want to ask about that bookcase. Nice to have met you. Bye."

When they were out of earshot Mark asked, with a grin and a wink, "And who was that?"

Katrina turned to him smiling broadly and replied, "That's my next door neighbour in the new house. He brought me dahlias from his garden on the day I moved in, to welcome me. He's taking me out to supper on Saturday. Isn't that nice?"

Mark gave her a quizzical look but said no more. He had noticed how flustered his mother had looked, talking to Charles. He hoped he would make her happy. She deserved a bit of fun.

That evening Katrina was left alone as Mark and Sarah set off for supper with Peter. She suddenly felt very lonely in the empty house. She put on the television, but found herself dozing off so decided to give herself an early night. It had been a busy couple of days and she slept so soundly she didn't even hear Mark and Sarah coming in. Next morning she crept into their room to say goodbye, before going to work, and stood looking at them for a while before disturbing them. They were certainly a handsome couple. She was sad to think that they would be gone by the time she got home.

CHAPTER TWO

When Katrina arrived at the shop that morning she found Sue in a bad mood.

"You don't seem very happy this morning," she remarked. "Anything I can do to help?"

"No thanks. I'm just having a few problems at home," Sue retorted. "Just mind the shop and I'll get some office work done."

With that, she disappeared into the back room with a clipboard and Katrina was left to wonder. It was not a busy day but a few customers wandered in and Katrina helped find clothes for them and give advice without having to call for help. She felt rather pleased with herself.

As Sue was locking up that evening a rather scruffy teenager, dressed all in black, arrived on the doorstep. Sue greeted him and turned to Katrina saying, "This is Darren, my son. Darren this is Katrina, she helps me in the shop."

The boy mumbled "Hello", after glancing quickly at Katrina and stood awkwardly by, waiting for her to go so that he could talk to his mother. Katrina took the hint, said goodbye to Sue and went off to find her car and drive home.

As she drove, she wondered again about Sue's private life. She now knew that Sue had a son, but what about a husband or partner? He had never been mentioned, but then Katrina had never really had a talk with Sue about anything other than work. Anyway, she told herself, it was none of her business.

Next day the shop was busy again, and by 5.30 Sue and Katrina were both feeling exhausted. It came as a surprise to Katrina when Sue suggested that the two of them should go for a drink on their way home. Katrina agreed but said she musn't be too long as she had a date for supper.

"Alright for some," remarked Sue grinning broadly. She had definitely cheered up during the day. They settled themselves down with their coffee at a quiet table in the local Bistro and Sue lit a cigarette.

"Ahh," she said, after inhaling deeply. "I needed that. I'm sorry I've been a bit tetchy for the last couple of days but I am having a bit of a problem with Darren. He's a darling boy really and I love him to bits but he can be a real handful at times. Do you mind listening to my woes? It would be so nice to have someone to talk to."

"Not at all," replied Katrina. "Fire away."

"To begin at the beginning, five years ago, when Darren was twelve, his Father walked out on us. Up till that time he had been a well balanced well behaved child but suddenly all that changed. I had to go to work full time as my ex was paying us no maintenance, and I suppose I was not around as much as I should have been for Darren.

"He started playing truant from school and not doing his homework, until at last the headmaster asked me to go in and have a talk about it all. I explained the situation and said I would talk to Darren. After that I tried to find more time for him and talked through his feelings about his father leaving. I also explained why I had to be away working so much. Then I pointed out that it was important for him to get a good education so that he would be employable when he left school.

"In spite of all my efforts he still managed to leave school at sixteen with no qualifications and no ambition to do anything at all. He even managed to get caught shop-lifting. Being arrested and taken to court gave him a bit of a scare, I think, so he hasn't tried that again but he is still just drifting about getting nowhere. It's an awful worry."

"Pity we can't find him anything to do at the shop."

"Oh, he was very good when I first got the shop. He was a great help cleaning up and decorating but I can't think of anything else he could do now."

Katrina thought how lucky she was that her two children were settled and she didn't have a bored teenager to deal with.

"I'm sorry that I can't be more helpful," she said lamely. "Aren't there any courses Darren could do, to train him for some sort of work?"

"He tried to get on one of those, to learn car maintenance, but it was full by the time he applied. I just wish there was something he was really interested in. I have to hope that he suddenly gets inspired by someone or something. He's got a good brain, if only he would use it. I'm very afraid that he is going to get into bad company again. Do you have any children?"

"Yes, a boy and a girl but they are both much older than your son, and settled thank goodness. Penny is married with two children and Mark works in London."

"Lucky you," said Sue looking at her watch. "Well, it's time we were getting home. Thanks for listening. Have a lovely evening. I shall look forward to hearing all about it on Monday."

Katrina drove home worrying that she was not going to have much time to change before her date with Charles. Luckily she had laid out her best black sheath dress with shoes and jewellery ready for a quick change, before she went to work. In the end she surprised herself and was quite ready by the time he rang the doorbell. She felt rather nervous as she went to answer it. Many years had passed since she last went out on a date. Should she ask Charles in for a drink or just grab her coat and go? She decided on the later, and opened the door with her coat on. There he stood on the doorstep looking very handsome, in a dark blue suit, pale blue shirt and navy and red tie.

"Good evening Katrina. You look gorgeous, if I may say so."

"Thank you," she said, doing a nervous little curtsey. She felt a blush creeping up her face. She hoped Charles hadn't noticed.

"Shall we go then?" he said grinning broadly. She followed him across the road and, as elegantly as possible, slid her self into his little sports car. This was the life, she thought, being taken out to supper by a very handsome man in a Porsche. She could hardly believe it.

After a rather terrifying drive through the countryside they arrived at the restaurant. It was obviously a very smart place and Katrina was pleased that she had worn her favourite black silk dress. The head waiter greeted Charles like an old friend and they were quickly shown to their table. They ordered cocktails and began to study the enormous menus. Katrina had been given a special guest

24

menu with no prices on, which she thought was a nice touch. She decided to start with smoked salmon, followed by duck. The waiter arrived with their cocktails and took their orders.

When he had gone she sat back in her chair and looked around. The restaurant was elegantly decorated and full of rich looking, beautifully dressed people. It was a long time since she had been taken to anywhere quite so opulent.

"What a beautiful place this is," she said to Charles. "I feel utterly spoilt."

"Glad you like it," he replied. " I must say one can always depend on a really good meal here, and the ambiance is good too, don't you think?"

"Gorgeous. Do you come here often? The waiter seemed to know you."

"Now and again. Good waiters have good memories. Now, tell me how are you getting on with your new job? You hadn't started when we last talked and were a bit nervous about it."

"I am enjoying it very much, thank you. It can be very busy at times and other times it can get a bit boring, but on the whole I love it. My boss, Sue, is good to work for and we seem to be getting on really well now. She was a bit aloof at first but now we are good friends. What kind of work do you do?" she enquired, determined to find out more about this handsome man.

"I work as a bodyguard, that is to say I look after important and famous people who might be under threat from attack of some kind. It's an interesting job, one never knows where one will be from one minute to the next, but it can play havoc with the social life. I was married once but my wife got so fed up with my sudden disappearances that she divorced me in the end. She designs clothes for the rich and famous, and felt I should be giving her more support socially. I hated big parties of rich people and usually managed to get sent on a job when one was coming up. I think she walked out in the hope that I would toe the line, rather than loose her, but I'm afraid I called her bluff. We are still good friends. She lives in London and I live here and we meet when it suits us, no pressure, a comfortable relationship."

The waiter arrived with the starters and as Katrina was being served, she couldn't help wondering if Charles usually came here with his ex wife. It put a bit of a damper on her enthusiastic mood.

As they ate their delicious meal Katrina asked Charles more about his job. She had never met a bodyguard before.

"Is it very dangerous?" she asked. "Do you have to carry a gun and learn self defence? I bet you are jolly fit."

Charles laughed. "Yes, it can be dangerous, yes, I do have to carry a gun and I do have to practise self defence and yes, I do keep myself very fit. I also have frequent medicals to make sure I am up to the job. All these things keep the risks down to the minimum. As I said before, the big problem is when jobs come up suddenly and I just have to drop everything and go, no matter what other plans I may have."

Katrina was silent for a while, thinking of the implications of what Charles had just said. Finally she grinned at him and said, "Your job must be a perfect excuse for getting out of things you don't want to do."

"Yes, perfect," he replied and they laughed. "As we are on to our life histories, may I ask about the father of your children?" he enquired.

Katrina took a deep breath. "His name is Peter and he left me about a year ago. He is now married again, to a girl called Shirley, who used to be his secretary. We're not good friends; in fact, I dread meeting him. He still lives locally but we move in different circles, so on the whole it is not a problem. We don't fight or anything, I just feel angry with him for treating me badly, and walking out after twenty seven years, rather unexpectedly, I might add."

"I see. Hence the move and the job I suppose. Sorry to upset you, but I was just interested."

"That's all right. I'm a lot less upset than I used to be, at least I don't burst into tears all the time, like I used to."

The waiter came with their meals at that moment and the awkward mood was broken as they ate and chatted about safer subjects. Later, when their food had been eaten and their coffee drunk, they left the restaurant, got back into the Porsche, and drove home through the dark lanes. Katrina felt slightly drunk after all the wine and sat back in her seat, wondering how the evening would end. Should she ask Charles in for a nightcap? Charles parked the car in his drive and helped her out. They walked together to her doorstep, where she fumbled for her key in her bag.

"Thank you for a marvellous evening," she said when she had found it and put it in the door.

"Thank you for coming and being such good company. We must do it again sometime." He gave her a quick peck on the cheek and turning, walked down the drive. Katrina felt rather deflated. She had hoped Charles would at least come in for a nightcap. She let herself in and went up to bed telling herself not to be so silly.

In spite of Katrina's hopes to the contrary she saw nothing of Charles for the next few weeks. She supposed he was working in some exotic location and hoped he was safe. At the shop, she and Sue were becoming firm friends. They often had a meal together after work and talked through their various problems. Sue got very excited when Darren found himself a job at last, in the local Tescos. The two friends were having a meal at the Bistro one evening when Sue told Katrina the news.

"Darren met this girl at a disco he went to with some of his mates. He seems to have fallen for her in a big way. Anyway he told her he was on the dole and she said she had heard of a job going at Tescos, where she works too apparently, so he actually got up early and went for an interview. Surprise, surprise he got the job. It's only stacking shelves, but it's a start. I'm so thrilled."

"Oh Sue, I'm so pleased for you. As you say it's not a very exciting job but if he works hard, it could well lead to other things. Let's have another glass of wine to celebrate."

Some days later, Katrina was tidying the shop when Mrs Benson, one of her old aquaintances from her committee days, came in.

"Ah, Katrina," she said, bustling across the shop to where Katrina was hanging up some clothes. "I was hoping I would find you here. How are you?"

"I'm fine thank you. Did you want some help to choose some clothes?"

"Not at the moment, no, there is something else I wanted to talk to you about. We have just had a committee meeting and want some new ways of fund raising. How do you feel about doing a fashion show for us?"

Katrina was a bit taken aback. "It's not up to me," she replied. "I only work here. Have a seat and I'll go and find my boss and see what she says."

Sue's reaction was one of amazement when Katrina told her of Mrs Bensons idea. She thought about it for a while and then said, "OK, why not? It will be good advertising for us at any rate. I'll be through in a minute, I'll just finish here."

So it was arranged that in the early spring of the following year the shop would do a fashion show. When Mrs Benson had gone Sue said, "This is going to be an awful lot of work, you know. I hope we don't regret getting involved."

"I'm sure we will be all right. We could ask my daughter Penny to help, and Darren, and the new girlfriend."

Sue laughed. "With your enthusiasm to keep us going, I'm sure we shall be fine," she said, giving her friend a hug.

The weather during the first week in October was wonderful and Mr Pan's garden was looking magnificent. Katrina phoned the nursing home to see if she could take him out for tea. She collected him one sunny afternoon and took him to visit his garden. He walked round with Katrina giving her advice on pruning and compost, thoroughly enjoying himself and being very bossy. Finally, when he was quite sure she knew how to proceed, they went indoors for tea. Conversation flowed well at first but suddenly they seemed to run out of things to say. Katrina was quite relieved when the door bell rang and she could get up and answer it.

"Charles," she exclaimed, surprised and happy to find him on her doorstep, "Come in, come in. I've got a friend of yours here, I'm sure you'd love to see."

Charles followed her into the room and greeted Mr Pan with great enthusiasm. Katrina left them to it and went out to make more tea. Suddenly it was 5.30 and time to take Mr Pan back to the nursing home. It had been a most successful afternoon and Katrina was rather proud of herself. Charles came back with them in the back of the car, chattering to Mr Pan all the way. When they arrived, they helped him out of the car and back to the big dining room, where supper was just being served.

"Just in time for my next meal," he laughed. "Thank you for a lovely afternoon both of you. Goodbye."

Charles and Katrina felt dismissed. As they left they could hear Mr Pan telling his friends about his excursion.

"It was so nice to give the old fellow an outing and show him that I am looking after his precious garden," mused Katrina. "It took very little effort and seemed to make him very happy."

"You're a good soul," proclaimed Charles. "Now, how about a meal at the Bistro as a reward?"

"What a lovely idea," she replied, and turned the car towards town.

They had a good meal and while they ate Charles told Katrina all about his latest trip, to South America. He was an amusing and informative storyteller and Katrina thoroughly enjoyed his company.

At the end of the evening he once more left her on her doorstep with a peck on the cheek and no arrangements to see her again. It was all very platonic.

She was woken next morning by the phone ringing. It was Sue.

"Sorry if I woke you," she apologised. "I know it's not one of your working days but could you meet me at the shop and look after it for the day? Darren's in the hospital and I need to be there with him."

"Oh dear. What's happened?" asked Katrina, full of concern for her friend.

"He's been involved in an accident. I'll tell you all about it when I see you. Can you come?"

"Yes of course. I'll just throw some clothes on. See you in about half an hour."

She got dressed and drove down to the shop. She let herself in and found Sue sitting at her desk, with her head in her hands sobbing. She looked up as Katrina came in and looked very relieved

29

when she saw who it was. Katrina led her into the back room and made her some coffee.

"Now tell me what is going on," she demanded. "You look as if you have been up all night."

"I must say I have been up since very early. The police phoned me in the early hours to tell me that Darren had been involved in a car crash and was in hospital. It appears that he, and a few of his mates had stolen a car and gone for a joy ride. The driver, not Darren, took a corner too quickly and spun the car, ending up crashing into a tree. Darren was in the front and his head hit the windscreen. They think he may have cracked his skull. I have to go back to the hospital and talk to the doctors about the x-rays. God, I feel awful. I really thought Darren had settled down, and now this. At least no one was seriously hurt but they will all have to go to court about taking the car."

Katrina tried to think of something to say to comfort her friend, but could think of nothing. Poor Sue looked a complete wreck, quite unlike her usual smart self.

"Oh Sue, I'm so sorry. Don't worry about the shop anyway. I've no special plans for the next while, so I can hold the fort as long as you like. Just leave me the name of the hospital and Darren's ward, then I can contact you if I need to."

Sue wrote the details down on the pad for Katrina. Then she took a deep breath and set off again for the hospital, insisting she was quite alright to drive.

That evening, as Katrina was shutting up shop Sue phoned. "Well, the good news is that Darren has not cracked his skull, so I am taking him home now. Can you work tomorrow again? I don't want to leave him by himself for the moment. He's very shaken. I want to have a long talk with him and see why he suddenly went off the rails again."

"Don't worry. I can easily do tomorrow in the shop. You look after Darren, and get some sleep."

"Thanks Katrina. You're an angel. Bye."

As it turned out Katrina ran the shop for the next three days with no special problems, other than at the end of her stint she was quite exhausted. She was very glad to see Sue back and hear that

30

Darren was thoroughly recovered. His excuse for his misdemeanour was that he had had a nasty row with the new girlfriend and had got very drunk. He felt he was not fully responsible for his actions and had broken into the car for a dare.

"I can sympathise with his reasoning, but heavens knows how the judge will feel, when he has to go to court," worried Sue. "By the way, I have met the girlfriend at last. She has a shaved head and a stud through her nose and her clothes are really strange, but basically she is a very charming girl. She gave Darren a real talking to about the joyriding. It's great, - he really takes notice of what she says, which is more than he does when I talk to him. I'm glad to say they seem to have made up their quarrel too."

"Apart from the court case everything is back to normal then. Great."

Over the next couple of months Katrina's life settled down into a routine. She went out to supper with Sue from time to time and learnt more and more about her life. Now and again Charles would turn up and whisk her off in the Porsche, which was always great fun. However, the relationship still remained very casual and platonic with no more than a peck on the cheek on the doorstep after a date. At the beginning of December Katrina started thinking about Christmas. She decided she had better phone her children and ask them over for Christmas day. She phoned Mark and he promised to bring Sarah. Once again she was amazed and thrilled that the two of them were still together. The length of the relationship must be some sort of record for Mark. Next, she spoke to Penny who also accepted her invitation and asked Katrina over for Boxing Day with her.

Lastly she thought about Charles. Should she ask him or would he hate a houseful of people, including two small boys. She asked Sue what she thought.

"Nothing ventured, nothing gained I say," replied her friend, so she took her courage in both hands and went to visit Charles that very evening. He took ages to answer the door and as she was about to leave and try another day, he appeared with the telephone in his hand.

"Katrina, how lovely to see you. Go through, I'll just finish this call and I will be right with you."

She went through to the sitting room and made herself comfy on one of the big chairs. The coffee table was covered with papers and a small laptop computer. She had obviously interrupted Charles in the middle of his work. She heard him put down the phone and come through to join her.

"Now, how about a drink," he said collecting up the papers and clearing the table. "Wine suit?"

"Sorry, I seem to have interrupted you in the middle of something. Don't let me hold you up. I just came to ask you if you would like to join myself and my family for Christmas lunch. It might be a bit hectic, but I would hate to think of you here all alone."

After a slight hesitation, during which time Katrina thought he was going to say no, he replied, "That's really kind of you. Yes, I would love to come. I haven't had a family Christmas for years."

"I'll look forward to seeing you then," she said getting up. "I'd better go now and leave you to get on."

He saw her to the door and she returned home feeling delighted that he had accepted her invitation. It was going to be a great Christmas.

The shop became really busy during December. Apart from all the people buying new outfits for parties, lots of others came in looking for presents. Sue had foreseen this and brought in more jewellery, scarves and lovely little decorated boxes of all sizes and shapes. They all went like hot cakes and Sue was delighted. The shop had been running for about nine months now and at last it seemed to be making her a living. She was still very worried about Darren's court case, but it was not scheduled till February so she was trying to forget about it for the moment.

On Christmas Eve Sue and Katrina shut up shop after another busy day, and decided to go for a drink, before going home. They settled in a corner of the warm, crowded pub and Sue proposed a toast, "Here's to a Happy Christmas to us both, and thanks Katrina for working so hard."

"Happy Christmas," replied Katrina. "And thank you for being such a friend. What are your plans for the holiday?"

"Well, tonight I am going to a party, held by one of my neighbours. Should be a good laugh, she's a hoot and has some very lively friends. On Christmas Day Darren and Tracy are coming for lunch. I just hope my hangover is not too intense."

They laughed together and swapped stories about terrible Christmases they had spent in the past. By the time they had finished their second drinks, they were both feeling light headed and decided it was time they went home, before they became incapable of driving. As they were leaving Sue said, "Have a wonderful Christmas Katrina, don't do anything I wouldn't, with that Charles of yours. See you New Year's Eve, in the shop about 10, OK? We'll sort out the clothes ready for the sale."

"Yes, fine. See you then. Bye."

Katrina drove home very carefully hoping she would not meet a policeman. What with a busy day at the shop, excitement over tomorrow and two glasses of wine she felt quite tipsy. She rolled the window down and sang carols, loudly, all the way home.

Next day she was up early to get the turkey in the oven and get the house ready for her guests. Penny and her family were the first to arrive. Max and Josh couldn't wait to show her the presents they had.

Their mother tried to calm them, but it was a losing battle. The carpet was suddenly covered with cars and trains and books, produced from large bags they had carried in with them. Katrina got down on her knees and admired everything she was shown.

She looked up at James and Penny and said, "If you two want a drink I should help yourselves. I seem to be a bit tied up." They laughed and helped themselves as directed.

Next to arrive were Mark and Sarah, looking rather windblown, having driven from London with the roof down. Having greeted everyone and got themselves drinks they too joined the party on the floor.

Finally Charles arrived, looking as handsome as ever, and was introduced to everyone and given a drink. When he had settled down to talk to James, Katrina and Penny slipped out to the kitchen to finish off the lunch.

"That Charles of yours looks more gorgeous every time I see him," said Penny, putting on the potatoes to boil. "How is the grand affair going then?"

"I wouldn't call it a grand affair exactly," replied her mother. "We are just good friends."

"Pull the other one. I don't expect you notice the way he looks at you. There's definitely a spark there somewhere," insisted Penny, winking at Katrina in a knowing way.

"Well, we'll see," she replied, trying to stay calm and casual. Deep down she prayed that her daughter was right but it was no good getting false hopes.

The lunch was a great success. The meal was delicious, the little boys behaved perfectly and everyone else got on well and chatted amongst themselves. When it was over everyone helped to clear away and then it was time for presents.

Max and Josh, with the help of their mother, distributed the bright parcels they found under the tree. Katrina had bought Charles a bottle of Malt Whisky, which she knew he liked and got a thank you kiss for her pains. He then produced from his pocket a very small, beautifully wrapped parcel and gave it to Katrina. She unwrapped it very carefully and found inside a pair of exquisitely made silver earrings.

"Oh, Charles, how beautiful, thank you." She kissed him and everyone crowded round to look in the little box.

"I do hope you like them. They come from Mexico. I saw them in a shop window when I was over there and thought they would suit you."

" I love them," exclaimed Katrina taking out the pearl studs she was wearing, and putting them on. She went over to the mirror to admire them. "Aren't they just perfect? Thank you, Charles."

Charles beamed. "Glad you approve of my choice."

Now that all the presents were opened the grown ups began to clear up all the paper and ribbon strewn about the floor, while the children played on the floor with their new toys. When everything was tidy again, they all decided a walk in the park would be nice. Katrina took her camera and managed to get a group shot. Then Charles took the camera and took a picture of the family. It was amazingly mild for December and the sun shone and Katrina felt that she had not been as happy as this for an awfully long time. As she walked along with Charles he said, "Thank you, Katrina, for asking me today. I must say I did have qualms about coming. I'm not used to family get togethers and felt I might feel a bit of an outsider. However I needn't have worried. Your lovely family has made me feel so welcome. The only problem is that it has made me feel very sad that I have no children, no family of my own. Usually having no ties is a bonus for me, but today I have become very jealous of what you have here."

"Don't get the idea that it is always like this," replied Katrina with a smile. "We have terrible fights sometimes you know. Anyway, I am really pleased you have enjoyed the day. We have all certainly enjoyed having you." She felt very happy that Charles had enjoyed her little family. She had a terrible urge to dance round on the grass to show how happy she was, but she knew her children would be embarrassed at her mad behaviour so she restrained herself. The light was beginning to fade and it was getting chilly so they all turned for home. They all felt refreshed by the walk and were hungry for tea.

By nine o'clock everyone except Charles had gone home and he and Katrina sat by the fire, staring into the flames and sipping Whisky. Katrina didn't want him to leave so in spite of her feeling of exhaustion she asked, "Can I get you some more food? There's plenty of turkey left for a sandwich."

Charles turned away from the fire and looked deep into her eyes. A thrill went down her spine and she held her breath as he said, "Food is the last thing on my mind at the moment. Oh Katrina, I think I am falling in love with you."

He took her in his arms and kissed her with a passion that overwhelmed her. She returned his embrace with equal passion and slowly he began to undress her as they moved onto the rug in front of the fire. He made love to her gently and courteously, bringing her to a climax that shot through her body like a red hot spear. They lay together on the rug at last, spent and peaceful, entwined in each other's arms.

"You have no idea how long I have wanted to do that," he said, pulling away at last and looking into her eyes. "I was so worried about hurting you, after all the problems you have had with

Peter. I can give you no stability, no quiet domesticity but I can give you love and friendship and companionship if that will do."

"That will do me very nicely, thank you," she said, with mock primness. "Would you like to stay the night, or am I being too forward? I should so love to find you there when I wake in the morning."

"You are just a brazen hussy," he replied teasingly. "But I must say, the idea does appeal."

They laughed together and without more ado collected up their clothes and went upstairs, giggling all the way. They got into the big bed and made love again, before falling into an exhausted sleep.

Katrina woke with a start in the morning and found herself alone in the bed. Had last night been a marvellous dream? At that moment Charles entered the room, wearing her dressing gown and carrying a tray of breakfast. Katrina got a fit of the giggles; Charles looked so funny in her blue silk dressing gown. It was much too small for him.

"If you are going to laugh, I shall take this breakfast straight downstairs again," said Charles in a haughty voice.

Katrina put her hand over her mouth and tried to stop laughing. Charles put the tray down, and taking the dressing gown off, stood before her quite naked. "That better?" he enquired. Katrina gazed at his muscular body, with her head on one side and felt her body becoming aroused all over again.

"Put yourself away," she laughed. "Otherwise I shall be forced to attack you and then the breakfast will be wasted."

"Who needs food?" he asked, as he jumped into bed with her, covering her naked body with kisses.

It was late morning by the time they eventually got up, and the breakfast lay untouched by the bed. Katrina was upset that she had arranged to go to see Penny, but as it turned out, Charles had a lunch date with friends as well, so they kissed and parted and promised to get together again soon.

Later, as Penny met her mother on the doorstep she gave her a quick kiss and whispered, "What have you been up to? You look glowing this morning."

"Tell you later," she replied as her two grandsons burst onto the scene, vying for attention.

Penny gave her a quizzical look and said, "Can't wait."

It was another lovely family day for Katrina. James's parents were also visiting for the day, so Penny was kept busy looking after her guests and was not able to talk to her mother alone until the boys were in bed and James's parents had left. James was happily watching the television, so mother and daughter sneaked out to do yet more washing up and have a good chat.

"Now Mum," began Penny. "Let's have the low down on what you have been up to."

"I don't know quite how to put this," faltered Katrina. "Basically Charles and I fell into bed together last night."

Penny took her mother in her arms and gave her a big hug. "Oh Mum, I'm so happy for you. I told you he fancied you didn't I?"

"You're not shocked or anything, then? This kind of thing is all new to me. I've never slept with anyone but your father before. It was so wonderful, I'm in a bit of a daze today."

"Should I get a new hat for the wedding?" Penny asked giggling.

Katrina stared into the distance and said, "No, I don't think so. It's early days yet but I somehow don't think there will be a wedding."

"When are you seeing him again? Oh this is exciting."

"We have no special plans. His work takes him away a lot, we shall see."

Just then James came into the kitchen looking for ice for his drink, so the subject was dropped. Katrina thought that Penny would talk to him later, when they were alone, in case he was shocked. One never knew these days.

For the next few days Katrina tried to keep herself busy to keep her mind off the fact that there was no word from Charles. At first she was sad, then she was cross that he hadn't even bothered to phone her. On New Years Eve she went into the shop to meet Sue and found it a great relief to have something to do. The two friends worked through the day getting things ready for the start of the sale the next day.

"When this sale is over," said Sue, wearily, "we are going to have to do some stocktaking I'm afraid. I hate the job but it's best to do it when the stock is low, as you can imagine. Do you mind doing a few extra hours again?"

"Not at all. No problem."

"Good, thanks. Now let's go off to the Bistro, shall we? I think we deserve it."

As they ate their meal Katrina asked Sue about her Christmas. Apparently it had not been as bad as Sue had feared. The party on Christmas Eve had been great fun and Sue had staggered home in the early hours. Luckily her hangover had not been too severe and she was very proud of the meal she had cooked for Darren and Tracy on Christmas day. After the meal they had talked and played silly board games and watched the telly, till it became yet another late night. Since then time had hung heavily on Sue's hands and she was glad to be back to work .

"Now, Katrina," she enquired. "How was Christmas for you?"

Katrina told Sue the whole story, how wonderful Christmas day had been, especially the night, and how Charles had now completely disappeared.

"I feel used," she said. "My beautiful bubble has burst just like that."

"That's men for you," said Sue cynically. "They are not to be trusted. I must say I really thought that you had a good man with that Charles, though. From your description he sounded a real gentleman. Just shows, you never can tell."

CHAPTER THREE

January came and went and there was still no word from Charles. The really frustrating thing was that Katrina had no one to ask about his whereabouts. She didn't know where he worked, she knew he had an ex-wife in London called Sonja but she didn't know where she lived. She knew his parents were dead and he had no siblings. All this information was no help to her whatsoever. She thought over all the possibilities in her head, but could find no reason for him not to have phoned her, at least. On the other hand what right had she to know what he was up to?

He probably said, 'I think I am falling in love with you' to all the girls he went to bed with; who knows? Then there was Penny's remark at Christmas, that she was sure he was crazy about her. It just didn't add up. Sue was her usual cynical self and advised Katrina to forget all about him and stop worrying. Katrina found that quite impossible.

One morning as she was cleaning her house, and thinking about Charles as usual, she suddenly had an inspiration. Charles had a cleaning woman once a week. Maybe she would know where Charles was and what was going on. Before she had time to lose her nerve, she stopped what she was doing and went straight next door. As luck would have it, she had chosen the right day. Mrs Daley, the cleaning lady, opened the door to her and asked her what she wanted. She was a big woman and Katrina felt rather intimidated.

"Good morning," she began tentatively. "So sorry to bother you. My name is Katrina Blackwell and I live next door. I have been trying to contact Mr Harris and can't seem to catch him," she lied. "I was wondering if you knew where he was and when he would be back."

Mrs Daley looked her up and down for a moment then deciding she was trustworthy said, "Sorry luv, I can't really help you. Mr Harris comes and goes all the time, sometimes he tells me where he's going and sometimes he don't. This time he didn't. It's his job you know, he sometimes leaves in a bit of a hurry. Tell you what I'll let you know if I hear anything, all right, dear?"

"Thank you very much," said Katrina disappointed that her inspiration had got her nowhere. She went back to her house and got on with her work, still unable to get Charles out of her thoughts. At least Mrs Daley had insinuated that he was away somewhere and therefore hadn't just stood her up. That at least made her feel a bit better.

As Katrina's love life evaporated, Sue's took off. She had met a man called Patrick at a party on New Years Eve and had fallen for him, hook, line and sinker. He was good looking, charming and seemed to have plenty of money. Sue was thoroughly enjoying being wined and dined and taken away for weekends. Katrina felt very happy for her friend. She deserved a bit of fun.

One evening Patrick came to the shop to fetch Sue for yet another jaunt, and as Sue changed in the back room Katrina had a chance to speak to him. He seemed pleasant enough, but she got the strange feeling that there was something not quite right about him. He was just too charming to be true. She prayed that she was wrong and Sue would not be hurt again. She had enough to worry about at the moment, with Darren's court appearance looming in mid February.

A few days later Katrina returned to her house, after a days shopping, and found a letter waiting for her on the mat. It was an airmail envelope with a Bolivian stamp on it. She turned it over in her hands, wondering who she knew in that part of the world. At last she opened it and read the typed page.

Santa Cruz,
Bolivia,
14.02.97.

Dear Mrs Blackwell,

I am a hospital visitor at the main hospital in Santa Cruz. Mr Charles Harris, one of our patients here, has asked me to write to you. He wants me to tell you that he is safe and will soon be well enough to be flown home to England. He will contact you again when he is back. I hope this letter has put your mind at rest.

Yours Sincerely

Sally Black.

Katrina read the letter through again and felt her heart pounding against her ribs. All this time she had been trying to forget Charles while he had been lying sick in some hospital in Bolivia. She felt the tears running down her face as she stared at the piece of paper in her hand. She wanted to speak to Charles, hold him in her arms and comfort him, but she didn't even know where he was. She started pacing the room, holding the letter close to her chest, as if it would bring her nearer to him.

She decided to phone Penny and dialled the number with a shaking hand. She tried to sound as calm as she could.

"Hello Penny. This is your mother. Can I come round? I have had a bit of a shock and need someone to talk to."

"Mum, you sound awful. You stay there. I'll be round in a moment and you can tell me all about it."

Katrina paced the room again as she waited for Penny to arrive. She felt so useless. She wanted to do something for Charles, but that was impossible. At last she heard the car in the drive and went to let her visitor in. She grabbed her daughter to her and hugged her tight, feeling a bit of comfort at last. They went through to the sitting room.

"You look awful, let me get you a nice glass of whisky," said Penny going over to the cabinet, "then you can tell me what on earth has happened."

Mother and daughter sat in the big chairs, sipping their drinks and Katrina went over the contents of the letter.

"Oh Mum," exclaimed Penny, when she had finished. "What a shock for you. The letter is so minimal, what a pity it didn't go in to more detail. It's dated a week ago. Charles could be on his way home by now. Maybe he will phone tomorrow and you will be able to find out what is going on."

Katrina began to sob again, "I feel so awful about the nasty thoughts I had about him, when all the time he was sick and unable to get in touch," said Katrina through her tears.

"Don't blame yourself! You weren't to know what was happening. It's strange that it has taken him so long to get in touch though, and why didn't he write himself? It's all a bit of a mystery isn't it? Now do you want me to take you home with me tonight or would you prefer your own bed?"

"Thanks for the offer but I think I would rather stay here. I have to go to work tomorrow anyway and it's easier from here."

"Are you sure you are OK for work? I'm sure Sue would give you the day off, in the circumstances."

"I think I would rather be at work. Take my mind off things."

"Whatever you say. I'll ring again tomorrow and see if there is any news." She suddenly had an idea. "Why don't you write to Charles at the address on the letter? It won't do any harm and at least you would feel you were doing something," she suggested.

"Well, I could do I suppose," replied her mother uncertainly. "As you say, it won't do any harm."

"He'll be home soon, I'm sure, then all will be revealed. Until then I don't think there's anything else you can do. I wish I could think of something." She went and sat nearer to her mother and put her arms round her, rocking her as if she was one of her children who needed comforting. At last Katrina pulled away and blew her nose loudly.

"Sorry to be such a pain," she apologised. "Come on, it's getting late. You had better get back to you family. Thanks so much for coming over."

Penny kissed her mother goodbye and drove off into the night. She wished she had been able to do more.

Katrina sat up in bed and wrote a long letter to Charles. Penny was right, it did make her feel better. She took a sleeping pill, in spite of having had the whisky, and eventually dozed off. She had strange dreams that night, about Charles, bandaged like a mummy, floating away so that she could not reach him. She woke with a headache and dragged herself to work.

42

She told Sue about the letter and her friend apologised for all the nasty things she had said about Charles during his disappearance.

"If you want any time off to go and visit your man when he gets home you have only to ask," she said generously.

"Thanks. I may have to take you up on that."

"Now to get back to business. Last night I had a call from your Mrs Benson, about the fashion show in March."

"Ah, yes," said Katrina trying to put her thoughts of Charles away for the moment.

"She has hired a hall for the last Friday in March. Now we need some models, eight I thought. I will ask a few of the customers but I wondered if your daughter would be interested. I thought two young girls, late teens, early twenties; four women, late twenties early thirties and two mature women of about fifty. What do you think?"

"Sounds fine to me. Would the models work in pairs, only I was thinking maybe Penny would like to bring a friend."

"That would be great. Darren, if he is not in jail by then, says he will do some music for us. He has a friend who has amplifiers and so on, so I will leave that to him – for the moment anyway. Will you come with me and look at the hall sometime? We need to see the layout and plan some kind of catwalk."

"Yes, of course. It all sounds rather fun," said Katrina pleased to have something new to think about.

"It's jolly hard work actually, but fun too. I must say I am rather looking forward to it."

That evening, when Penny phoned to see how she was, Katrina told her about the fashion show.

"I told Sue I would see if you would be willing to be a model and perhaps bring a friend. What do you think? You have such a lovely figure."

"Flattery will get you everywhere," laughed Penny. "I'll tell you what, I'll ask Prue if she can come and give me moral support and then let you know OK?"

"That's fine, but don't leave it too long, please as there is not a lot of time if we have to find someone else."

"OK Mum, I'll get back to you as soon as I can. Let me know if you hear anything from Charles won't you? Did you write a letter?"

"Yes I did and felt better for it. Thanks for the idea. I'll let you know if there is any news. Bye."

Three more days went by with still no word from Charles, then suddenly one evening, there he was at the other end of the telephone saying, "Good evening Katrina. How are you?" as if he had been down the road to buy a paper.

"Oh, Charles. Where are you? How are you? What happened? Oh, I am so pleased to hear your voice, you have no idea." Katrina stopped for breath.

"To answer your questions in order, first, I am in hospital in London, second, I am feeling much better thank you, and third, the story is too long to tell on the phone. When can you come and see me?"

"How about tomorrow? When's the best time?"

"Tomorrow afternoon would be best I think. Oh Katrina I have missed you. I can't wait till tomorrow. Have you missed me too?"

"Oh yes. I wrote you a letter, when I got the one from Sally Black, but I don't expect you got it if you are in England already. I have been worried to death about you. I shall look forward to hearing the whole saga when I see you. Can you give me some directions?"

Charles gave her the name of the hospital and the ward he was in and then told her how to get there.

"Must go now," he said finally." See you tomorrow. Sleep well."

Katrina sat for a while staring at the phone then dialled Penny's number to tell her the good news.

Next day Katrina travelled up to London. It was an easy journey and she arrived earlier than she had expected, so she had a cup of coffee and a Danish in a little cafe near the hospital. The closer she got to Charles, the more she worried about what had happened to him. If he was badly injured how would she cope with it? Would she still feel the same way about him? It was therefore with some trepidation that she eventually went into the side room that the nurse pointed out to her, when she arrived in Charles's ward.

She needn't have worried. There was Charles sitting up in bed, looking as handsome as ever, if a little paler and thinner than when she last saw him. She put down the flowers and grapes she had brought and rushed across to give him an enormous hug.

"Oh Charles, it's so wonderful to see you again," she exclaimed, then untangling herself she stood back and said, "I think you are playing for sympathy. You look right as rain to me."

There was a long silence during which Katrina wished she had not made her last remark. A terrible sadness came over Charles's face as he looked down at the bedclothes, pulling himself together ready to tell Katrina what was wrong with him.

"Perhaps I should begin at the beginning and tell you the whole story," he said looking up at last. Katrina sat on the bed side chair and waited. Charles continued, "On Boxing Day I was called away in the middle of the party to go on a job. It entailed travelling to Bolivia with a businessman, who had some important work to do out there. It was all very annoying, but part of the job. It was only supposed to take a few days, so I thought I would be back before you could miss me. As my charge and I were being driven from the airport at Santa Cruz, the hire car was stopped at gun point and we were taken hostage. We were driven, blindfolded, for what seemed like miles, then we were taken out of the car and locked into a small room, still blindfolded, for two weeks. We were fed by the guards but otherwise saw and heard nothing. It was ghastly as you can imagine. I have never been so terrified in all my life. We thought we might be shot at any moment. Time meant nothing to us, as it was always dark behind the blindfolds, and we got terrible cramp in our arms from being tied up. After two weeks we were rescued by the police. A gun battle ensued and I was shot in the shoulder, caught in the cross fire. Apparently it was all smashed to pieces. They did what they could to patch it up in Bolivia but it is still a mess. I can't use my right hand at all. It's quite dead."

Charles's face suddenly crumpled as he began to weep, covering his face with his left hand. Katrina took him in her arms

45

and stroked his head trying to comfort him. It was all like a bad dream to her, in a minute she would wake up.

"I'm sorry, I'm sorry," Charles kept repeating as she continued to comfort him. At last he was all cried out. Katrina sat back in her chair as Charles blew his nose rather loudly and tried a weak smile.

"Sorry about that," he said as he lay back on his pillows exhausted.

"Can this hospital do any more for you?" asked Katrina, wanting to know everything.

"Well, they are operating tomorrow afternoon to see what can be done. I feel there must be some chance or they wouldn't bother. Could you still love me with one arm, do you think?"

"Course I could," insisted Katrina, trying not to think about the possible problems ahead.

The nurse came in with some tea and they sat drinking and chatting until it began to get dark outside the windows. Katrina was beginning to feel totally exhausted and told Charles it was time she was getting home. She hated travelling at night by herself. Charles quite understood and thanked her for coming and being such a comfort. "I would like to keep you all night but I don't think it's allowed somehow," joked Charles, getting back to his usual cheerful self. "Will you phone tomorrow?"

"Yes, of course. What time is your op?"

"Two, I believe, so phone in the evening. I should be awake by then."

"OK, I'll do that then. Good luck tomorrow. I'll walk about with my fingers crossed all day."

They hugged each other for a long time. Katrina wished she could just crawl in beside him and make love to him all night, but that would have to wait. On the way home on the train she went over and over what Charles had told her about his ordeal. She was amazed how well he was coping. She wondered if he had nightmares.

When she got home, Katrina phoned Penny again to give her an update on Charles. She told her about the kidnapping and could hear Penny gasping on the other end of the line. Then she told

46

her about the shoulder injury and the paralysis and the op the next day.

"Did you speak to any of the doctors?" Penny asked.

"No, there were none around. Maybe next time I go up I'll try."

"How do you feel about a Charles with one arm?"

"I really don't know yet. I'm sure there will be problems but I shall do my best to work them out as time goes by. I still love him, but if he gets too angry about his lot, I may not be able to cope. I do hope I can, but it's going to be hard if this op doesn't work."

"Well, you know where we are if we can help in any way. Oh, I nearly forgot. Prue and I would love to do the fashion show. Can you tell Sue?"

"That's great news, Sue will be pleased. Well, I'll leave you in peace now. Thanks for listening. Bye."

The following evening, after a busy day at work, Katrina phoned the hospital to find out how Charles's operation had gone. It took her ages to get through to the ward, and she got more and more nervous as she waited. At last she got through to the Sister in charge.

"Hello," she said. "This is Katrina Blackwell. I am phoning to find out how Mr Charles Harris is doing after his op today."

"Are you a relative?" asked the Sister.

"No, just a good friend," replied Katrina.

She could hear the Sister at the other end of the line shuffling papers. At last she said, "Mr Harris is comfortable. That is all the information I can give you I'm afraid."

"You make it sound as if there is a lot more to tell. Can't you give me any more details?"

"I'm sorry. As you are not a relative I can't go into details with you."

Katrina began to feel very cross. This was ridiculous. She needed to know whether the op had been a success but the Sister was adamant. She could give no further information. At last Katrina gave up and vowed to try again the next day. Maybe she would speak to someone more amenable.

That night she took another sleeping pill, but still woke in the early hours worrying.

47

Sue threatened to send her home again when she got to work that morning.

"You look ghastly," she said seeing Katrina's pale face. "Do you want the day off?"

"No thanks, Sue. I'd rather have something to do. Sitting alone and thinking does me no good at all. I just wish the hospital would tell me what is going on. I've decided that if I can't get any sense from them tonight, when I phone, I shall go up tomorrow and visit and try and find a doctor to talk to."

"Good idea. Now if you insist on staying, lets go and get some clothes sorted, shall we?"

That evening Katrina phoned the hospital again, but got no further than she had the night before. Charles was comfortable and that was all they would tell her. When she rang off she got out her timetable and checked on the times of trains for the following day.
She arrived at the hospital, in the early afternoon and went up to the ward. She was greeted by one of the nurses and asked who she was visiting.

When she said, "Charles Harris," she was asked her name and told to sit in a side room and wait a moment, as the doctor wanted to speak to her. After what seemed to Katrina a very long time a very young, harassed looking doctor arrived and, shutting the door behind him, sat down next to her.

"Good afternoon, Mrs Blackwell. So sorry to have kept you waiting. I'm Dr Andrews, one of the surgeons who operated on Mr Harris on Friday. I'm afraid the news is not good. We took a good look at the injured shoulder and I'm afraid there is nothing more we can do. The nerves have been shattered by the bullet he received and they are beyond repair, mainly because it is such a long time since the accident. We are giving him Physiotherapy but it is of limited use I fear. Our problem now is that Mr Harris has taken the news of his condition extremely badly. I gather he was a very active man and the loss of movement in his right arm makes him feel that life is not worth living.

"I gather that you are a very special friend of his, and as he seems to have no other living relatives, I am going to ask your help in trying to convince him that his life is not over. He has told the

48

nurses that he doesn't want to see anyone or talk to anyone. He won't even leave his room or take any phone calls. We could get a councillor in to speak to him but he refuses to cooperate. We are pinning our hopes on you. Do you think you can cope?"

Katrina sat back in her chair, stunned at what Dr Andrews had said. She was going to have an enormous task on her hands. Would she be able to cope? All she knew was that she loved Charles, in spite of everything, and hopefully he loved her enough to listen to her. She took a deep breath and said, "Thank you for being so honest with me Dr Andrews. Strangely I feel better now that I know everything. I love Charles very much and will do everything in my power to make him see sense. I am no psychiatrist but I shall do my very best."

Dr Andrews beamed at her. "Well done," he said. "I can see why Mr Harris is so fond of you. You are quite a lady. Now, I think your best plan is to go in to see Charles and not say anything about our little conversation. I don't want him to feel we are talking about him behind his back. Play it by ear. Good luck. I think you'll need it."

Katrina walked down the ward to Charles's room with her heart pounding in her ears. He was lying in his bed staring up at the ceiling, a look of total defeat on his face. She went across the room and sat on the chair by the bed. She took his hand and although he didn't pull it away he didn't look at her, but continued to look at the ceiling.

"I told them I didn't want any visitors," he protested. "Can't you just leave me alone?"

"Well, that's a fine welcome," she retorted. "I've come all this way to see you and all you can do is sulk. For goodness sake, talk to me." She was surprise at her own anger.

"You don't understand," he said, still not looking at her.

"Explain it to me then. Help me to understand."

At last he turned and looked into her eyes. Katrina had never seen so much pain on a face.

"I'm a cripple. They can't do anything for me. My right arm and hand are dead and they are never going to get any better. My life is finished, I may as well be dead."

49

"Don't be so dramatic Charles. Of course your life isn't finished. You just have a bit of adapting to do. It will probably take a long time but I still love you and will help you all I can. Please, Charles."

"It's easy for you to say. You have two good arms."

"Another thing. They say that there is nothing they can do for you now, but who knows what new operations they will be able to do in the future. There is always hope, Charles."

He turned away and Katrina was afraid that she was not going to get through to him. What else could she say? Suddenly he turned back to look at her and her hopes rose.

"Did you mean what you said? Could you really still love me?" he asked.

Katrina stood up and took him in her arms. She felt the tears creeping down her face.

"Oh, Charles, darling, of course I still love you, you foolish fellow. Why do you think I have come to see you, for goodness sake?"

Charles hugged her against his chest and she could feel its spasms as he sobbed into her hair. They stayed entwined for a long time, until at last he was calm again. Katrina pulled away and gave him a tissue to wipe his face. She felt as if she had been through a storm of emotion and now they were through it and all would be well – for the moment anyway. She realised there would be other storms for her to deal with, but hopefully never as bad as this one. She felt quite drained. She took Charles's hand again and they sat there for a long time deep in their own thoughts. An orderly came in and offered them tea and they accepted it gratefully.

"Actually, I would prefer a stiff drink," said Charles as they drank . "Unfortunately there seems to be no bar here." They laughed.

"When do you think you will be able to come home?" Katrina asked.

"No one has said yet, and I have been too miserable to bother to ask. It will be marvellous to be in my own bed again. I feel as if I have been in hospital beds forever."

"Tell them, when you get home I will be quite happy to do whatever is necessary to help you out, shopping, cooking and so on. Maybe that will speed up your discharge."

"Thanks, darling. I'll tell them, though I hope to be independent as soon as I can. I hate the idea of being reliant on anyone."

"That's the spirit. Make plans, look forward. Have you heard from the people at work? What is the situation there?"

"My boss came to see me when I first arrived here. He was full of condolences for what had happened. I will get a lump sum of money, because my injury was received in the line of duty, so I won't be on the bread line. However, I said I would be grateful if he could find me some kind of job in the office, as I shall go quite crazy if I have nothing to do. He said he would see what he could do and get back to me, but I have heard nothing more. Mind you, I have been refusing to take calls." He took her hand and squeezed it. "Katrina, how can I ever thank you for talking me into seeing sense? I feel, with your support I can at least try to build up some kind of life for myself. I was so scared that you wouldn't want anything to do with me now I am crippled, and I have no one else. No parents, no children, friends yes, but friends who play squash, golf, sail boats and drive fast cars. I don't think I could fit in with them any more."

"Perhaps, now you are feeling a bit better, you could go out into the ward and talk to some of the other patients. I'm sure sitting around by yourself thinking and worrying isn't going to help you."

"Darling Katrina, ever practical. What have I done to deserve you?"

He pulled her to him and kissed her passionately. Just then the nurse walked in to take Charles's temperature and was pleased to see that he was getting some good TLC.

Katrina dozed on the way home in the train and nearly missed her station. She was very glad to fall into bed that night, and was asleep as soon as her head touched the pillow.

Next day in the shop she told Sue all about her visit to Charles. It was wonderful to have someone to talk to about her hopes and fears for the future. Finally she said, "I think he is over the worst now, and beginning to face up to the fact that he has just got to

51

rearrange his life to cope with his disability. I've done the best I can, now it's up to him."

"He's so lucky to have you there, Katrina. It's going to be an awful strain on you I'm afraid. When are you going up to see him again?"

"Wednesday, I thought. I think I shall lay in bed all day tomorrow and catch up on some sleep."

"Good idea. You look as if you could do with a rest. You need to look after yourself if you are going to help Charles."

Katrina phoned the hospital on Monday and Tuesday evenings and had long talks with Charles. The nurses had obviously been told to put her straight through. There was no nonsense about not being a relative any more. There was no special news yet about his discharge so she arranged to go to see him again on Wednesday.

When she arrived on the ward, she found Charles talking to one of the other patients. Katrina was introduced and they talked a little before retreating to Charles's room where they fell into each others arms.

"I have missed you Katrina," said Charles breaking away at last. "Now we had better sit down and look respectable. The nurse will be in with the tea soon and we don't want to get caught snogging again. We will get a reputation."

They laughed and sat down and began to give each other their news. Charles still didn't know when he would be allowed home. His wound was slightly infected so he had to stay until that was settled. He had phoned around to see if there was any chance of him ever being able to drive again. As things stood at the moment it would be illegal for him to do so apparently. If he had two arms and no legs, they could adapt his car, but one arm was dangerous. It was a bitter blow. Charles loved his Porsche, now he would have to sell it. The afternoon shot by and soon it was time for Katrina to leave. She promised to phone the next day and see how things were. On her way out she bumped into Dr Andrews again.

"Hello Mrs Blackwell. How are you? Satisfied with the patient, I hope. Well done for making him feel that life was worth living again. You did a great job. Apparently you will be willing to keep an eye on him when he gets home."

"Yes, of course. I only live next door so it will be no problem."

"Good. We just want to get this wound of his healed, then we shall throw him out. Shouldn't be too long."

"Thank you for looking after him so well. It will be nice to have him home again, though."

"Yes, I'm sure. Well, I must be off. Bye."

In the end it was another two weeks before Charles was allowed home. Katrina went to London in the car to collect him in a great state of excitement. She had spent the previous few days spring cleaning Charles's house and stocking his fridge ready for his return. He was thrilled with the result.

"My goodness," he said, looking round. " I have never seen the place look so clean. Thank you so much. What a gem," he pulled her to him and held her so tight she had problems breathing. "It's so wonderful to be home at last. Yippee." He danced round the room with her until they became breathless and fell onto the settee to recover.

When they had got their breath back Katrina suggested they went back to her house and she made them some supper. After the meal they sat and talked and felt utterly at peace with the world. Finally Katrina asked, "Will you be all right by yourself tonight do you think or would you rather stay here?"

"No I'll be OK. I've got to get used to dealing with things on my own. The occupational therapist at the hospital has been giving me lessons on how to manage one handed. It's really not too difficult. I think I had better go now. It's getting late and I am whacked. You must be too. Thank you for coming to bring me home, Katrina," he said, getting up.

They kissed on the door step and Katrina watched him go down the path. She hoped he would be all right.

Next day she had to go into the shop as Sue was going to court with Darren. His case was due at eleven but Katrina was not expecting to see Sue for the rest of the day. However just after one, Sue burst into the shop looking furious. Katrina was serving a customer so Sue went straight into the back room to put on the kettle. As soon as Katrina was able, she joined her there.

"What on earth happened?" she enquired. "You look about to burst."

Sue drew deeply on her cigarette and replied, "I don't believe these people," she raged. "We got to the court just before eleven, we sat around for ages waiting for the case to be heard. At last we were called, only to be told that the lawyer had asked for an adjournment and we have to go through the whole thing again in a month. Seems to me its just a fiddle so that the fat lawyer gets yet another fat fee. It's not fair. My nerves are in shreds and now we have to start again."

"How's Darren taking all this?" Katrina asked.

"Oh he's as cool as a cucumber. He's gone back to work as if nothing had happened."

"Did the lawyer give you any idea what was likely to happen to Darren?"

"He thinks he will probably get a suspended sentence, but one never knows. Tracy came to give moral support, by the way, wasn't that nice?"

"Good for her."

"Now enough of my problems. How's Charles?"

Katrina told her friend all about bringing Charles home.

"He's got my number here in case he gets into difficulties but he is pretty determined to be independent. The district nurse is coming in this morning to do his dressing, so that will be a diversion. We shall just have to play it by ear. May I have tomorrow off do you think? I should like to take him out in the fresh air. He's been in hospital too long and he's looking very pasty."

"Yes, of course, no problem. Thanks so much for holding the fort today. By the way what happened about Charles's job?"

"He is hoping to get a desk job of some kind as time goes by. He's been awarded a lump sum because of his injury, so he doesn't need to work, he just needs something to do."

"I can understand that. It was a rather exciting job he had and he must be very bored sitting around."

"Yes, this is the big problem. Let's hope his old firm find him something soon."

When Katrina got home that evening she went straight round to see Charles and ask him to supper. He took a long time to answer the door, and Katrina guessed that he had been asleep. He looked very tousled.

"Ah, Katrina," he exclaimed." Are you back from work already? I must have been asleep. Come in."

She followed him into the sitting room.

"I came to ask you to supper," she said. "Have you had a good day?"

"Not really. The nurse came and did my dressing, but I haven't seen another soul. I have been bored and lonely and frustrated that I can't do things properly. I dropped a whole bottle of milk over the floor and then cut my finger trying to pick the pieces up. It's been a nightmare. I don't know if I can live like this." He put his head in his hands. Katrina put her arm round him, but he shrugged it off.

"Come on Charles," she said sternly." This is your first day on your own since the accident. You knew it wouldn't be easy. It's all going to take time. Anyway, tomorrow Sue has given me the day off, as I worked today, so I can be with you all day. We can go out if you like, drive around and have lunch somewhere nice."

"You seem to have forgotten that I am a cripple and can't manage a knife and fork properly. There is no way I can eat in public. You would have to cut everything up for me."

"Do you mean to tell me that you are never going to eat in public again? Don't be so silly, Charles. You have got to face this problem in the end, why not tomorrow? Americans seem to manage to eat most things with a fork, why not you? Steak could be a problem I agree, but what about omelettes, cottage pie, lasagne to name but a few. Come on Charles, it's a challenge."

Looking up at last, and grinning broadly he said, "You have an answer for everything don't you? I think you just enjoy bossing me about. I thought those hospital nurses were authoritarian but you're worse. OK then, I accept your challenge. Tomorrow we shall go out for lunch. Just one thing, let's eat somewhere a long way from here so that if I make a real hash of it, no one I know will be watching."

"OK that's a deal then. Now how about some supper at my place?" suggested Katrina, happy that they had managed to get over yet another problem. "You can get in some practise for tomorrow with cottage pie."

"Oh God, slops again," he exclaimed teasingly.

"Don't you call my cottage pie slops," she replied sternly, "or I shall withdraw my invitation."

"Come here," he said grabbing her with his good left arm. "I want to show you how much I love you."

She giggled and happily surrendered to his kisses. Supper was eaten rather late that night.

Next day it rained heavily and the drive was not as pleasant as Katrina had hoped. However they found an inviting looking pub at last, miles from anywhere, and enjoyed a very pleasant meal. Charles chose the lasagne and managed it perfectly well with his left hand.

"See," said Katrina when his plate was clean. "I told you you could do it."

"OK bossy boots, you win," he replied with a grin. "Now, how about pudding?" The sun was shinning by the time they drove home so they found a nice spot, stopped the car and walked for miles, happy in each others company. There were going to be problems for a long time yet, but at least Charles was coming to terms with his disability more and more each day, thought Katrina. She squeezed his hand and thanked her lucky stars it was only his arm that was damaged, after all he could easily have died.

CHAPTER FOUR

As the days went by, Charles began to get more and more confident. He often went down to the pub for his lunch, if Katrina wasn't there, and he even went up to London to visit his boss, to ask again about some work. When Charles had first come home Katrina had spent most of her time with him, when she was not working, but gradually she found he was doing more and more on his own. His wound healed well and the district nurse stopped coming, so all his time was his own.

He refused to let Katrina go on cleaning his house, insisting Mrs Daley was perfectly capable. The big woman thoroughly enjoyed fussing over him, as if he was one of her own children, and now did all his washing as well as her cleaning duties.

One evening, Katrina was sitting alone watching the television when there was a ring at the doorbell. She thought it was probably Charles, home from his dominoes match at the pub, and was therefore amazed to see Darren standing there on her doorstep, looking rather unwell.

"Hello," she said. "Come in."

"Can I use your toilet?" he asked, and rushed towards it as she pointed the way.

'Just in time,' thought Katrina, as the sound of vomiting issued from the loo. She went into the kitchen and got a glass of water ready for him, when he had finished.

At last he joined her in the sitting room, looking as white as a sheet and very embarrassed. Katrina got up and gave him the water.

"Now, Darren, sit down there and drink that water very slowly and tell me what on earth has happened."

He sat down, clutching his glass, looking very sheepish.

"I'm so sorry," he said sitting back in his chair and taking a deep breath. "I didn't know who else to turn to."

"What about your mother?" asked Katrina feeling very sorry for him but wondering why on earth he had come to see her. She hardly knew him.

"My mother would kill me if she found out. You won't tell her will you?"

"I'm making no promises until I find out what has happened," retorted Katrina.

"I've lost the money and I wondered if you could lend me some. It's very urgent and I thought you could help perhaps."

"Darren, you are not making sense. What money have you lost?"

"The money Chris and I have been saving."

"Who is Chris, and what were you saving for?"

"Chris is a boy who works on Saturdays in Tescos with me. He's been helping me get the music ready for Mum's fashion show. We have decided to go into the disco business together, but we need some more equipment. We have been saving our wages, and Chris has had some money from his parents. Anyway, Chris found an advert in the paper and tomorrow we are supposed to be going round to see this second hand stuff and possibly buy it. This afternoon I went and got the money out of the building society ready to pay the deposit. Then I met a mate in the pub, who had a sure winner on the 2.30. Seemed a good way of making some more money so I put some on the horse. It lost so I tried again in the next race. That lost too, and so on. I'm now down £400. I just don't know what to do. I'm scared. Chris will kill me when he finds out. I had a few drinks and then suddenly thought that you might have some cash you could lend me. It's an awful cheek I know. I don't think I would have dared come if I hadn't been pissed." His words came tumbling out as if he felt he might loose his nerve if he didn't get it all said quickly.

"Now let me get this straight," said Katrina. "You spent the afternoon betting on the horses with money that partly belonged to Chris and you would like me to lend you £400 so that neither he, nor your mother, will ever know. As you say you have a bit of a cheek. How do you intend to pay me back?"

Darren looked more crestfallen than ever and stared at the floor. At last he looked up and said, "I don't know exactly," he admitted.

Katrina thought for a while, as Darren sat in his chair looking totally dejected. Finally she said, "I think you have been very foolish,

Darren, but then I'm sure you know that. I can understand your reluctance to tell your mother and I will try not to tell her either, though I refuse to lie to her if she asks me directly what happened. As for paying the money back I think I have an idea. Next door I have a friend who has just lost the use of his right arm in an accident. I know he has been looking for someone to help in his garden, so perhaps that is your answer. You could work a few hours a week for him, and he could pay me your wages. What do you think?"

"But I don't know anything about gardens," whined Darren.

"I'm sure Charles would be quite happy to teach you. Come on, have you a better idea?"

"No, I suppose not," replied Darren grudgingly.

"You never know, you might enjoy it, all that nice fresh air and exercise."

Darren grunted.

"Anyway," Katrina continued, "if these disco nights make you some money, you can give up the gardening and pay me off from the profits of those. Do you want me to speak to Charles?"

"I suppose so," said Darren uncertainly.

"Fine. Now, let's get down to business. Can you meet me in the bank tomorrow sometime?"

"I have to work till two but I could meet you about two thirty. Thanks Mrs Blackwell." He did his best to give her a smile but it was rather weak. He's quite exhausted, thought Katrina.

"Would you like some coffee before you go home?" she enquired.

"Yes please," he replied enthusiastically.

They went into the kitchen. Katrina gave Darren coffee and a piece of toast and the colour began to return to his face. Poor old Sue, she thought as she watched him eat, this boy of hers really knows how to get into trouble. When he had finished Katrina insisted on running him home in the car. She dropped him off at the end of the road, so that Sue wouldn't spot them. On her drive home she began to worry about whether she had done the right thing. How would she feel if Mark borrowed money from a virtual stranger rather than ask her? Oh well, it was too late now.

Next day Katrina went to the bank and drew out £400. She put it into an envelope and waited for Darren. She hoped the bank staff didn't think she was casing the place ready for a bank raid or something. She felt very clandestine. She was extremely pleased to see him at last. He had Tracy with him, so he must've told her about the money. When they reached Katrina Tracy said,"Thank you so much for helping Darren out, Mrs Blackwell. He's told me everything and I think you have been marvellous. Don't worry, I'll see he pays you back."

"Thank you, Tracy," she replied, thinking how lucky Darren had been to find this girl. Her appearance was always a little alarming, but she was bright and intelligent and if anyone could keep Darren in order, she could. She handed Darren the money. "Now please look after that very carefully won't you? I must be off now and get the shopping done. By the way, Darren, can you come round on Sunday and meet Charles? He's coming to lunch."

"OK then. Will 2.30, after work be all right?" He replied after a moments thought.

"Yes fine, see you then. Bye, bye Tracy."

As she went off to do her shopping, Katrina wondered if Tracy knew about the gardening. Perhaps she shouldn't have said anything about Charles in front of her.

That evening Charles came round to supper and she told him all about Darren and the money.

"You must be mad," he exclaimed. "I don't suppose you have a receipt for the money by any chance."

"No, I never thought to ask," she replied. "You're getting me worried now, Charles."

"It's no good worrying now, it's too late. He and Tracy are probably off somewhere making whoopee with your money, and you have no proof that you gave it to them."

"Oh Charles, what shall I do?"

He burst out laughing. "Don't worry. I am only trying to wind you up." Katrina hit him playfully.

"Seriously," she continued, "he's basically a very nice boy. He just gets into a lot of scrapes."

"You can say that again!" retorted Charles. "Will I be safe with him working in my garden?"

"Don't be silly, he's not that bad. You'll see on Sunday. Before long you will wonder how you ever managed without him."

"I hope you're right. Anyway we have spent enough time talking about Darren – I want to tell you my news now. They have found me a job. Isn't that wonderful?"

"Oh Charles," said Karina throwing her arms round him. "That's marvellous. When do you start?"

"On Monday next. Someone has gone off sick in the office so they phoned and asked me if I felt up to going in. I said I would give it a go."

"Do you want me to give you a ride to the station?"

"No, it's OK. I'll get a taxi. Stop fussing, woman."

"Will you come to supper then, after work, and tell me all about it?"

"Yes, that would be nice. I shall probably be quite exhausted with the travelling and will need looking after by then," he replied with a grin.

"You know I always enjoy doing that," she replied grinning broadly.

"Wanton woman," he exclaimed, holding her to him. "I do love you, Katrina."

Next day in the shop, Katrina longed for Sue to say something about Darren buying the disco equipment, then she would know that he had not just run off with her money. However she said nothing. Perhaps she didn't know. Katrina felt on edge all morning, frustrated that she couldn't ask Sue outright because she wasn't supposed to know anything. They were not busy in the shop so they started sorting the clothes for the fashion show. Katrina suddenly had an idea.

"What are you going to do about playing the music at the show?" she enquired, with baited breath.

"Oh, I shall use my tape recorder," replied Sue. "It has a mike attachment for me to use, so that should do. Darren is supposed to be bringing me a tape of the music, so that I can time it, but I haven't seen him for a couple of days."

Katrina's heart missed a beat. Perhaps Charles had been right. Sue looked up.

"Are you all right?" she asked. "You look worried all of a sudden."

"It's nothing," said Katrina trying a smile. "I just thought of something I forgot to tell Charles."

Sue gave her friend a funny look but luckily didn't pursue the point.

On Saturday evening Charles took Katrina to the cinema, to try and take her mind off Darren and the money. She had convinced herself that she was never going to see her £400 again. It was a good film, and for a while she got thoroughly immersed in the plot. She didn't often go to the cinema these days, so when she did it was a real treat. After the film they went to the Bistro for a meal.

"You're not with me this evening," accused Charles, as he looked across at Katrina, sitting upright in her chair, staring into space.

Katrina pulled herself back from her thoughts and said, "Sorry Charles. I can't get Darren out of my head. Silly isn't it? It's not as if I can't afford to lose the money it's just that I don't like to think I have been taken advantage of."

"The point is, there is nothing you can do about it now. He will probably turn up tomorrow, as planned, and you will wonder what you have been worrying about. Now here comes the waiter with our food. Let's enjoy it and forget about Darren for the moment shall we?" rebuked Charles sharply.

Next day Charles came round to lunch as planned. By 2.30 everything was washed up and put away but there was no sign of Darren.

"Perhaps he has forgotten," suggested Charles to Katrina, who was by this time pacing up and down. "As I said before there is nothing you can do now, just sit down and calm yourself."

"It's all very well for you," she replied tersely.

Half an hour later the doorbell rang and Katrina jumped out of her chair, where she had been trying to read the paper, and rushed to answer it. A great feeling of relief swept over her as she opened the door and found Darren standing there, quite oblivious of the worry he had caused her.

"Come in," she said, quelling the urge to hug him. "Charles is in the sitting room. Come through and I will introduce you."

"Thanks. Sorry I'm a bit late, but something cropped up."

They went in to the sitting room and Katrina made the introductions.

"Shall we all have some coffee?" she suggested, and when she got nods of approval she went off to the kitchen, leaving the two men to get to know each other. By the time she returned they were chatting away about Darren's plans for the disco business. Katrina served the coffee, then sat back and watched. She was so pleased that they seemed to have hit it off so well. Finally Darren looked at his watch.

"I think I had better be going now," he said. "I have to meet Tracy. Thanks for the coffee. I'll see you next Sunday then, Charles."

"I shall look forward to it. Let's hope the weather is kind. There's an awful lot to do."

Katrina showed Darren to the door.

"I'll probably see you on Friday then," she said. Darren looked puzzled. "At the fashion show," she reminded him. "You are coming to help aren't you?"

"Yes of course. See you then. Bye."

Katrina returned to the sitting room.

"Well?" she said to Charles, who was sitting deep in thought. "He's a nice boy isn't he? You seemed to be getting on very well with him."

Charles looked across at her and replied, "Yes, he seems to be OK. As you heard, he's coming next Sunday, after work, and we shall see how it goes. He admits he knows nothing about gardening but is willing to learn, so that's a start. I will pay him by the hour and pay his wages to you to pay off his debt. It's going to take a long time, I'm afraid, but as you said before, you're not desperate for the money."

"No, that's true. I was just so relieved to see him on the door step, you have no idea."

"I think I have. You have been really worried over the last few days, I know. Now that's over, how about a nice walk? I could do with a bit of fresh air."

They spent the rest of the afternoon walking in the park. Katrina felt as if a great weight had been lifted, now that the Darren business was settled. She felt at peace with the world.

On Monday two of the models for the show came in to try on their outfits. They were regular customers and thoroughly enjoyed trying on the clothes and practising their walks up and down the shop. It was arranged that they should be at the hall early on Friday night and have a rehearsal before the audience arrived. Sue was getting quite excited about the project. When they had gone she said, "Well, if all the models are as enthusiastic as those two we shall have a great time. Darren's music is perfect, I'm glad to say. Did I tell you he and his friend Chris have set up a disco business? Chris works with Darren on Saturdays in Tescos and knows a lot of people who are having birthday parties coming up and need music. He's still at school and a lot of his friends are about to be eighteen. He got the idea of setting up this business and asked Darren to help him. They have already brought a load of equipment and have their first gig next Saturday. It's all rather exciting. I do hope it all turns out OK. They are certainly very keen."

Katrina tried to look very surprised at Sue's news.

"How did they get the money to pay for the equipment?" she asked innocently.

"They've been saving up, apparently. I gather Chris has rather rich parents and I think they probably helped a bit."

"Good for them," exclaimed Katrina, stifling a smile. If only Sue knew the whole story.

That evening Katrina cooked a special supper for Charles. He came in at last looking exhausted and Katrina sat him down with a drink.

"Well, how did it go?" she asked. "You look a bit whacked out."

"I am exhausted. I had forgotten just how awful the rush hour was. I suppose I shall get used to it. Learning the new job was tiring too. Luckily I have a wonderful secretary who was most helpful, but there is an awful lot for me to learn. I've never had anything to do with the administration before. I've just taken my orders and got on with it. The best part of the day was having lunch in the local pub and meeting a load of old friends. They all said how much they had missed me. It was great. It was as if I had been accepted back into the family again."

"I'm so glad to hear that you are happy to be back at work. Mind you, I always knew you would be. It will all be a lot less exhausting when you get more used to it. Now how about some supper?"

Friday came at last and Katrina woke with a feeling of excitement. She arrived at the shop and found Sue putting final touches to her script.

"Morning," she said, looking up from her papers. "Could you just sit there and listen to this introduction a minute, and tell me what you think? I think it's alright but I would like your opinion."

Katrina sat down and listened while Sue read. When she was finished she said, "That sounds fine to me Sue. Is Mrs Benson going to make a speech too?"

"Oh yes. She's going to open the proceedings and then hand over to me. Now, can we just check all the prices, on this other list?" They went into the back room together and checked the prices on the clothes, then tied each model's outfits for the evening into a bundle and covered them with plastic protectors and labelled them.

"Well, that's a good job done," exclaimed Sue. "Now how about some coffee?"

At five o'clock they locked the shop and Sue went off to collect the van she had hired. When she got back they loaded all the clothes into it, with a few knick-knacks that Sue was going to put on a sales table, plus the tape recorder. They drove to the hall and found Mrs Benson and a few of her helpers already there, getting thing ready. They all helped to unload the van just as the first models were arriving. Sue told them to put on their first outfits, ready for the rehearsal, then she set up her tape recorder and microphone and tested it. The caretaker had already built a low catwalk down the centre of the room and everyone helped get out the chairs. The rehearsal was a bit of a shambles at first with the two models on the catwalk bumping into each other but they soon got the hang of it under Sue's guidance. Katrina went back to the dressing room with them just as the audience was beginning to arrive. Tension was rising, as the models checked their clothes and made sure their shoes and accessories were all in easy reach, ready for the quick changes. Katrina went across to speak to Penny.

"How are you feeling?" she asked. "You certainly look gorgeous."

"Thanks Mum. Actually I feel rather scared. It's all this waiting about. I shall feel better when we get going, I'm sure. Is it nearly time to go, do you think?"

"I'll go and see how things are going," she said looking at her watch. "Shouldn't be long now, darling. Good luck - or should I say break a leg?"

She went back into the hall and was glad to see Darren had turned up at last. He was sitting with his mother at the table, discussing the controls on the tape recorder. At that moment Katrina noticed Mrs Benson walk across the room to where Sue was seated. She was obviously ready to give her welcoming speech. Katrina went back to the changing room and asked the models to get into line ready to go onto the catwalk. Several of them looked very nervous, but they all looked wonderful in their clothes.

"Good luck everyone," said Katrina in a loud whisper. "When you come off again, change as quickly as you can and get back into line. Joan and Meg will be in the changing room to help you and hang up all the clothes when you take them off."

Sue finished her introduction and the music started. Penny and Prue, at Katrina's signal, swept through the curtain and onto the catwalk. The show had begun.

The next hour went in a flash. There was a good reaction from the audience all the way through the show, and the models gained confidence all the time. When it was all over Sue asked all the models to go onto the catwalk together and she introduced them to the audience by name and thanked them for their hard work. There was a resounding round of applause, as the models stood there grinning and looking very pleased with themselves. Mrs Benson made another speech thanking everyone, and announcing that the

66

clothes would be on sale as soon as Sue had sorted them out. Meanwhile there were wine and nibbles being served from the table at the back. Sue left Darren to clear up the tape recorder and the speakers and went into the dressing room.

"Well done, everyone," she said, beaming from ear to ear. "Thank you all so much for putting on such a great show. Kate Moss, eat your heart out. You all looked terrific. Now let's get these clothes on the racks and out to the punters."

Later, when most of the audience had gone and they were packing up, Charles arrived with a bottle of champagne "for the workers" as he put it. They all stopped what they were doing and toasted Sue, and each other, for a fine evenings work.

"Thank you so much for the champers," said Sue to Charles when everyone else had gone back to clearing up.

"I gather the evening was a great success," he replied.

"Yes, I think it was. Mrs Benson seems pleased with her takings and we sold quite a lot of clothes too. I must say though it's a relief to have it behind me. It's been a long time since I put on a show like that. I had forgotten how exhausting it was."

Next day Katrina and Sue were both very tired when they arrived in the shop. Sue took the van back, while Katrina began to sort out the clothes they had used for the show. She heard the bell go on the door and went back into the shop to see who it was.

She froze. There, sorting through one of the racks was Shirley, Peter's new wife. 'Why did this have to happen to me when I am alone in the shop?' she asked herself. She took a deep breath and as she stepped forward, Shirley turned round. The look on her face was a picture of surprise and embarrassment.

"I didn't know you worked here," she exclaimed, when she had managed to pull herself together.

Because of Shirley's obvious discomfort, Katrina suddenly felt very calm.

"Oh yes," she replied. "We abandoned wives have to find little ways to fill our time. Are you looking for anything special or just browsing?"

"Perhaps I shall come again another day," replied Shirley, and almost ran from the shop, nearly knocking Sue over, as she was coming in.

"Who on earth was that?" asked Sue as she closed the door. "She looked as if she had seen a ghost."

"That," said Katrina, grinning all over her face, "was the woman who stole my husband. She obviously didn't know that I worked here, and I'm afraid she got rather a shock when she saw me. She ran away! Wasn't that great? That has really made my morning."

"What a hoot! She certainly looked shaken. I just hope we haven't lost a good customer. Never mind, it was worth it."

Later, when the two friends were taking a coffee break, Sue said, "Thank you so much for all your help yesterday, Katrina. I do like your Charles. It was so nice of him to bring that champers. It's so sad about his arm. How is he coping at work?"

"He's getting very tired at the moment, but I dare say that will get better as time goes on. It's all the travelling and learning the new job."

"I hear Darren is doing some gardening for him."

Katrina was a bit taken aback. How was she going to explain it all to Sue without mentioning the money?

"Yes," she said, as casually as she could. "Charles said he needed some help and I thought Darren might like the extra money, so I introduced them. Darren is starting tomorrow, so I hope it all turns out OK."

She hoped she wasn't blushing, after all it wasn't a lie. She had just left out a few things. Sue gave her a quizzical look, but to Katrina's relief, didn't pursue the subject.

That evening Charles took Katrina out to supper. As they ate she told him about her day. Charles was most amused about Shirley, running from the shop.

"Well, you won't be worried about meeting her again," he remarked. "Just stand your ground and she will run. I wish I'd been there to see it."

They laughed and chatted through the meal and Katrina thought again how lucky she was to have Charles to look after her.

68

They were both very tired by the time they got back to Katrina's house for a nightcap. They decided on an early night, and after making love with their usual intensity, fell asleep in each other's arms, hardly moving until morning.

Next day, after lunch, Darren arrived to help Charles with his garden. Katrina was rather peeved that none of her windows overlooked Charles's garden and she couldn't see how they were getting on. She read the papers and waited, hoping that Charles would return and tell her how it went. It was nearly dark by the time he eventually arrived.

"Well?" she asked. "Is Darren going to be useful to you, or was my idea a no-no?"

Charles grinned at her worried face. "Don't worry," he replied. "Your idea was a great one. The boy worked really hard, and we had a nice chat. I think we shall get on fine. He's coming again next week anyway. Apparently his gig went very well last night, in spite of having to use some really old equipment, which was all they could afford. He and his friend Chris have great plans for the future, and it sounds as if they will make a go of it. Surely such enthusiasm can't fail."

"Oh Charles I'm so pleased you like him. Now he has all these plans perhaps he will keep out of trouble for a change."

"One can but hope," Charles retorted.

The following evening, as she was locking up the shop, Sue suggested that she and Katrina should go for a drink before going home. "There are a few things I should like to talk through with you," she explained.

Katrina's heart beat faster as she wondered if Sue had found out about Darren and the money. In a funny way, it would make things easier if she had. They sat in the pub with their drinks and Katrina waited with baited breath to hear what Sue had to say. She felt as if she was in the headmistresses room at school, Sue looked so stern and was drawing very deeply on her cigarette, a bad sign.

"I just wondered if you could manage to work the whole week by yourself, as from next Monday?" she began." I think you know the shop well enough now, and there's a clothes show on at

69

the Birmingham NEC that I should like to go to. What do you think?"

Katrina relaxed. "No problem," she replied. "I've got nothing special on next week. Charles is back at work now, so I only see him in the evenings anyway. Yes that would be fine. You'd better leave me a telephone number just in case there is a problem."

"Of course. Now there's just one other thing that's bothering me. What is the real reason for Darren doing all this gardening for Charles? There must be lots of people who could have helped him – why Darren? The only answer that I can come up with is that he owes you, or Charles, a favour. Did either of you lend him some money for this disco equipment?"

Katrina took a deep breath. She hated breaking her word to Darren but she could see no alternative. After all, Sue had pretty well guessed what had happened anyway. She proceeded to tell her the whole story and, as she had suspected, felt much better that it was now all out in the open. When she had finished Sue sat for a while deep in thought, then she said, "What I can't understand is why the little devil didn't come to me. I know we have our ups and downs, but basically I thought we could talk to each other about anything. I feel so hurt."

"Perhaps he thought that I had more money to spare than you. He must know that your finances are not all they could be, in spite of the fact that the shop is doing so well."

"I'm cross with you too for not telling me what had happened. I thought we were friends."

"Oh we are, Sue. Please don't let this interfere with that," pleaded Katrina. "Like Darren I didn't want to worry you. I hoped that you wouldn't find out then no harm would have been done, Charles would have a gardener and I would get my money back and that would have been that."

"Thanks for your concern," said Sue grudgingly, staring into her drink.

"Will you tell Darren that you know about the money?" Katrina enquired, feeling very bad that she had let both Darren and Sue down, with her do-gooding.

Sue looked up at last and replied, "I don't think I will. However if he lets Charles down and doesn't turn up to do the gardening, you are to let me know at once and let me deal with him, OK?"

"That's a deal then, I promise."

"Now lets talk about something else shall we? Can I get you another drink?"

The friends eventually decided to have supper in the pub and by the time they left Katrina felt that she had been forgiven.

Sue went off to Birmingham, as arranged, the following week and Katrina was left in the shop alone. By the end of the week she was exhausted, but pleased that she had managed and had not had to call Sue. On Monday morning they had a great reunion and Sue enthusiastically showed Katrina pictures and swatches of the clothes she had ordered.

"I went a bit mad," she admitted, "but everything was so gorgeous. The clothes will be arriving over the next few weeks so you will have a nice lot of steaming to do," she teased.

"Slave driver," Katrina retorted. It was so nice to have Sue back, she was surprised how much she had missed her.

"Now you are back Sue, can I ask a favour? Charles has a company dinner on a Friday in three weeks. Can I have Friday and Saturday off please? We thought we would stay over night in London after the do and make a weekend of it."

"Of course. How exciting. Where will it be held?"

"The Dorchester, I believe. Charles says not to get too excited about it, but I must say I find it rather difficult not to. There's to be dinner and dancing, but also, unfortunately, speeches. What a bore they can be! After a heavy meal and plenty of wine it seems like some kind of torture to have to listen to speeches."

"Seems to me a small price to pay for a good night out at the Dorchester."

"Yes, I'm just being silly."

"What are you going to wear?"

"I'm meeting Charles after work on Thursday and he is going to buy me a new dress. No offence, Sue, but I don't think there is anything quite suitable in here, do you?"

Sue put on a very pained expression. "My clothes not good enough for you, eh?"

Katrina laughed at the expression on her friends face. "Sorry, not this time Sue. You really can't complain though, most of my wages go on your clothes."

"I should hope so too. I give you a good discount don't I?"

"True. I'm looking forward to seeing these new clothes you have bought, the question is can I find an excuse to buy some."

"Course you can, if you put your mind to it."

Three weeks later, Katrina travelled up to London on the train to attend Charles' firm's Annual Dinner and Dance at the Dorchester. The dress Charles had brought her was wrapped very carefully and packed into a very large paper carrier at her feet. It was turquoise silk, shaped at the top and billowing into a magnificent full skirt at the bottom. She loved it and felt marvellous in it. It was so elegant and unfussy. It was probably very expensive too, but Charles refused to tell how much it had cost.

When she eventually arrived in London, she took a taxi to the hotel, where Charles had booked them in for the night. As the taxi arrived a doorman rushed across to open the door for her. She felt like a millionaire. She booked in and was taken up to her room. It was a nice big room with an ensuite bathroom, and the usual television, telephone and drinks bar. She unpacked and was glad to see that her dress was hardly creased. She decided to take a bath, so that it was free for Charles when he arrived, then she lazed on the bed and read the magazine she had brought for the train journey. As time went by she began to worry about what had happened to Charles, it was getting late. She started to change and do her make up, ready to put on her dress at the last minute. Suddenly the telephone rang. She picked it up and was relieved to find Charles on the other end.

"Hello Katrina. I'm sorry I've been held up at work and I haven't got time to get to the hotel. I shall have to change here. Can you get to the Dorchester alone? Get the doorman to get you a taxi, OK?"

Katrina was not at all happy about going alone but could see no alternative.

72

"All right," she conceded trying not to let her nervousness show. "What time should I get there? I don't want to get there before you."

"I'll be there in an hour," Charles promised. "I'm so sorry about this. I can't wait to see you again in that dress. I shall be the envy of the whole room with you on my arm."

"Charming as ever," laughed Katrina. "See you in an hour then."

She put the phone down and continued to get ready. She arrived at the Dorchester an hour later full of apprehension. She looked round the entrance hall but could see no sign of Charles. Everyone else seemed to be with a party of friends and she felt very alone. She began to feel very cross with Charles, putting her into this position. It was very unfair of him. She suddenly had a terrible urge to run away, and turned back towards the door. There stood Charles looking handsome and distinguished in his evening suit, searching the room for her. Just then he spotted her and moved through the throng of people to greet her. When he reached her he kissed her cheek and then held her at arms length saying, "Oh Katrina, you look fabulous. I'm so sorry I wasn't here when you arrived. Will you forgive me?"

"You arrived in the nick of time," replied Katrina sternly. "I was about to go back to the hotel and call it a day. I felt so out of place standing here all by myself, knowing no one."

Charles was a little taken aback by the reprimand, after all, he had only been a few minutes late.

"Well, I'm here now so lets get upstairs to the party, shall we?" he snapped.

The enormous room was full of tables, set out round a dance floor in the centre. Charles guided Katrina towards the bar. Their progress was slowed considerably, as Charles kept meeting friends to whom he proudly introduced Katrina. She began to feel a lot better and smiled sweetly at their banter.

When they had eventually got their drinks, they went in search of their allotted table. Katrina was pleased to find she was sitting next to Charles. So often at these dinners one was seated miles from one's partner. Next to her on the other side was Charles's friend Pete. They had known each other for many years and had often worked together in the field. Now they both had desk jobs.

"I am so pleased to meet you at last," he said as they were introduced. "I have heard so much about you. I thought that Charles was exaggerating when he said how beautiful you were but now I can see he wasn't. He's a lucky man."

Katrina felt very touched by Pete's speech and was annoyed to find herself blushing. Turning to Charles she said, "What charming friends you have. Do you all go to charm school?"

They all laughed. "Just you remember that you are with me this evening, Mrs Blackwell. Pete is an old married man."

Katrina was then introduced to Pete's wife Gloria and immediately took a liking to the rather loud, brightly dressed woman. The meal was delicious, and even the speeches weren't too long and boring, in spite of all the in-jokes that Katrina couldn't understand. The band arrived and arranged themselves on their little podium and the dancing began. Katrina found, to her delight that Charles was a very good dancer and she thoroughly enjoyed herself whirling round the floor with him. When he had first mentioned the dinner dance to her she had told him how much she enjoyed dancing and was quite taken aback when he had remarked that there was no way he was going to dance. People would stare, he insisted, when they noticed his arm hanging limply at his side. She had managed at last to persuade him not to be so silly.

"I'm sure people will have better things to do than stare at your arm," she insisted.

At first his arm had indeed been a bit of a problem. She tried holding it up to begin with, so that it rested on her shoulder but it was too heavy, so in the end she left it to hang by his side. It was much more comfortable that way and no one seemed to be staring. Several of Charles's friends insisted on a dance with Katrina and she hardly sat down all evening. She felt like the Belle of the Ball. Suddenly it was all over and everyone was arranging themselves in a circle ready for Auld Lang Syne. It had been a wonderful evening and everyone sang out with gusto. After a lot of goodbyes and promises to meet up again soon, Charles and Katrina took a taxi back to the hotel.

"Thank you for a marvellous evening," said Katrina as they took the lift up to their room.

"Not at all; thank you. I have never enjoyed a firm do so much in my life. You were right about no one noticing the dreaded arm. They had all had much too much to drink to care and I really enjoyed dancing again, especially with you, my little bossy boots," he said kissing her head.

The lift arrived at their floor and they walked down the corridor to their room.

"It's stupid I know," observed Katrina as they reached their door, "but I feel quite nervous and almost embarrassed going into a hotel room with you."

Charles put his arm round her, "Silly woman," he exclaimed. "Why is sharing a hotel room any different from sharing a room in our houses?"

"I don't know, it just is," insisted Katrina.

"You're not going to insist on a separate room are you?" he enquired nervously.

Katrina laughed at the worried look on his face. "No, don't worry. I shall be all right in a moment."

They went into the room.

"How about a nightcap?" enquired Charles, still worrying about Katrina's remarks.

"Yes, thanks. A small whisky perhaps."

They sat and sipped their drinks and talked about the evening, and slowly Katrina began to relax. When at last they got into bed she had forgotten all her feelings of apprehension and making love with Charles was as wonderful as ever, though she had to remember not to cry out, in case she could be heard next door.

They slept late the next morning and ordered breakfast in bed.

"Pure decadence!" exclaimed Charles. "You are leading me into bad ways, you wanton woman."

Katrina laughed and gave his stubbly cheek a kiss. "What shall we do today?" she asked. " Have you any plans?"

"No, nothing special. It looks a lovely day out there. Shall we take a river bus to Greenwich? We can walk off all that food and booze and have lunch in a pub."

"Good idea. I love Greenwich. I used to take the children there a lot when they were small."

"OK, we'll do that then."

Later they left their suitcases at the hotel and set off to find a river bus. The journey down the river was very exhilarating, as there was quite a stiff breeze blowing off the water to clear their fuzzy heads. They walked in the park and sat in the sun by the observatory, until they suddenly felt hungry and decided it was time to find some lunch. They walked across the park towards a pub that Charles knew well, which had tables in the garden and a good snack menu.

Suddenly behind them, a rather high pitched voice exclaimed, "Charles, fancy seeing you here!"

Charles whipped round to confront the owner of the voice. "Hello, Sonja. How unusual to see you walking anywhere," he remarked frostily.

"Aren't you going to introduce me to your companion?" she retorted, staring at Katrina.

"Sonja, this is Katrina Blackwell. Sonja and I used to be married, Katrina," explained Charles.

"Ah, how do you do, Sonja." The women shook hands, appraising each other as they did so. Katrina saw a tall elegant and beautifully dressed woman in a smart trouser suit. She had a look on her beautiful face as if she had just noticed a bad smell in her vicinity.

"Well, I won't stop you," Sonja continued, turning to smile at Charles. "Do come over sometime soon, won't you Charles. It's been such ages since we had a good talk."

With that she strode off, leaving Charles and Katrina staring after her.

"Sorry about that, Katrina," said Charles when Sonja was out of ear shot.

With some trepidation Katrina asked, "Do you see a lot of Sonja still?"

Charles looked rather sheepish and replied as casually as he could, "No, not a lot, but we do have lunch now and again. She likes to think I am still there if she needs me. Mind you she never once came to see me in the hospital. She hates illness of any sort. I'm a bit surprised that she has anything to do with me now that I'm damaged goods, so to speak. She's a strange woman."

They walked on in silence till they reached the pub. Sonja had put a shadow over the day, which had been so perfect till then.

As they sat waiting for their meal in the garden of the pub Charles said plaintively, "Please Katrina, don't let us allow that silly woman to spoil our day. There is really no need for you to be jealous of her. It is you I love, please believe that."

Katrina sat deep in thought for a while then replied, "I'm not exactly jealous. I just got the feeling that, given half a chance, Sonja would like to cause trouble between us. She gave me such an evil look. It was quite scary."

"Yes, I know that look well," chuckled Charles. "It's been aimed at me from time to time too. The main thing is never to believe anything she tells you. If she should get in touch with you and tell you stories about me, check with me before deciding never to see me again. She loves causing trouble."

"I'll bear that in mind," promised Katrina, though she still didn't feel totally happy with the situation.

CHAPTER FIVE

One afternoon in early May, a few weeks after their London trip, Charles and Katrina were sitting in her garden, soaking up the sun, when Charles suddenly turned to her and said, "Katrina, I have some exciting news for you."

"Goodness, that sounds interesting," replied Katrina opening her eyes and sitting up. "Well, go ahead. I'm all ears."

"I've been offered a job in New York, isn't that great?"

"New York," she exclaimed amazed.

"Yes, it would only be for six months. Would you come with me?"

Katrina's immediate reaction was to say no, but noticing the look on Charles's face she replied,

"Oh, Charles, can you give me a bit of time to think about this? It's a long way to go. What would I do with myself all day? I don't know anyone in New York."

Charles looked thoroughly dejected. He had been sure that Katrina would jump at the chance to go with him. Surely everyone wanted to see New York.

"I'm sure there's a lot to do over there, museums and art galleries to see, people to meet. There are lots of ex-pat wives who would be delighted to take you round, I'm sure. Would you be happier if we were married?" he added as an afterthought.

Katrina laughed. "That must be one of the strangest proposals on record," she declared. "Seriously though, it's nothing to do with being married or not. I just don't want to go and live in another country just at the moment. I'm settled here, after all the traumas of the divorce and the house move, and I simply can't face the idea of moving again."

"Not even with me?"

"Not even with you."

"I'm sorry, I misjudged your feelings Katrina," snapped Charles. "I thought we had a relationship going here, and you would want to be with me. Obviously I was quite wrong."

With that he got up from his chair, collected his things and left. Katrina was amazed at his behaviour, he was acting like a small boy who couldn't get his own way. She lay back in the sun and closed her eyes, there was no way she was going to chase after him. He would be back when he had calmed down she was sure.

Next day was Sunday, but there was still no sign of Charles. In the afternoon Darren came round looking for him as he could get no response from his house and wanted to get on with the gardening. Katrina lent him her lawn mower to do the grass, and hoped Charles wouldn't be cross.

In the shop the next day she spilled her heart out to Sue. She was beginning to feel thoroughly upset by the whole business.

"I don't know what to do," she explained to her friend. "I don't know where he's gone. I don't even know when he is due to go to America. He's behaving like a spoilt child."

"Personally I can't understand why you didn't want to go with him. I'd love six months in the Big Apple."

"Well, I suppose I'm just an old stick in the mud," Katrina retorted. "Suppose we fell out and I was left there all alone. I'm just not very brave. Sue, would you mind if I took a week off? I feel like a holiday to sort myself out. I just don't feel like sitting at home and waiting for Charles to phone."

"Of course. But are you sure that it's a good idea? What if Charles phones while you are away?"

"He'll have to try again when I get back," replied Katrina firmly.

"Well, if you're sure you aren't being a bit hasty, of course you can have the time off. I'm sure I can get someone to stand in for you. Where will you go?"

"I think Cornwall would be rather nice at this time of year, don't you?"

"I'm sure it would, but I still think you should give Charles a bit more time to get in touch. I still remember how upset you were when he was in Bolivia. Don't you care if you lose him any more?"

"Yes, of course I care, I just don't want to go to New York for six months. Charles would be working all day and I would just get lonely and bored. There are only so many museums one can visit

79

and stay interested, and as for taking lunch with a load of ex-pats every day, it is really not my scene."

"Takes all sorts, I suppose. I should love it," replied Sue, unable to grasp the problem at all.

The following day Katrina got up early and set off in her little car for Cornwall. She felt quite excited. It had been a long time since her last holiday, in France, with Peter, before her world fell apart. The rain bucketed down all the way and she hoped that this was not a bad omen. She arrived in Newquay in the early evening and drove around looking for somewhere to stay. As it was early in the season she managed to find herself a nice hotel, perched on a cliff above the sea.

By the time she had unpacked the rain had cleared and she decided to take a walk before supper. The air was fresh and clear after the rain and she breathed it in deeply as she walked. After a while she sat on the bench and just looked at the view. She could feel herself relaxing after the long drive as she watched the waves breaking on the rocks below. The problem of Charles and America still niggled at the back of her mind but for the next week she would put it on hold and enjoy herself. If she never saw him again she would survive, it would be heartbreaking after all they had been through, but it was not the end of the world. Perhaps she was being stupid but she felt very strongly that she did not want to go to New York and that was that. Finally she got up and wandered back to the hotel.

She had never been holiday by herself before and eating alone in the big dining room was not a pleasant experience, in spite of the good food. Tomorrow I must bring a book to read as I eat, she thought to herself. She felt very alone as she watched the families and couples at the other tables laughing and joking as they ate their meals. She began to wonder if it had been a mistake running away from her problems like that. The feeling of peace she had found sitting on top of the cliff had evaporated. Here she was, all alone, with too much time to think, and no one to talk to. After the meal she decided to have a drink in the bar, before going up to bed. Perhaps it would help her sleep. She ordered a whisky and carried it to an empty table. As she sat down, she found she was being followed by a small, elderly lady, with a round, smiling face and a twinkle in her eye.

"May I join you?" she enquired smiling sweetly.

Katrina smiled back. "Of course," Katrina replied moving to make room for her new companion.

The little lady sat down. "I noticed that you were eating alone in the dining room," she explained. "I thought you might like some company. I hope you don't mind."

"Not at all. It's nice to have someone to talk to. I'm Katrina Blackwell, by the way."

"How do you do? I'm Emily Mills. Are you staying here alone?"

"Yes. I've never been on holiday alone before. I think eating alone is the worst of it, don't you?"

"Yes, I agree. I've been here three days now and you are the first person I have seen on their own. Maybe we could get a table together."

"That would be nice. I was thinking I would have to bring a book to the dining room with me tomorrow, so that I wouldn't feel so isolated amid all the jollity at the other tables. Now I won't have to bother." Katrina suddenly hoped that she would not regret agreeing to share a table with her new acquaintance, after all, this little woman could turn out to be a real bore. Oh well, it was too late now.

"Have you been here before?" asked Emily.

"No. I just drove down here on spec and found this place as I was driving round. It's a lovely spot isn't it?"

"Yes. I love it here. I used to come with my husband. He died last year, and at first I wondered if it was a mistake to return alone. There are so many memories. Now I am glad I came. The staff have been so kind. Have you any plans for your stay here?"

"No, not really. I thought I would do some walking perhaps, if the weather behaves."

"Would you mind if I tagged along? Do say if you want to be alone."

"No, it would be nice to have someone to talk to, especially if you know the area. You can give me some ideas of where to go. Do you do a lot of walking?"

"Not as much now as I used to, but I do love it. I have this silly theory that if you keep yourself moving you don't seize up so quickly in old age."

"You're probably right," agreed Katrina. " You certainly look very fit."

"Shall I order a packed lunch for tomorrow?" enquired Emily, changing the subject.

Katrina suddenly felt that she was being organised by this little woman. Did she really want to spend the whole day walking with her? On the other hand she didn't want to upset her new friend, and she didn't have any other plans. After a short pause she replied,"Yes, that would be fine. If the weather looks too bad we could go for a drive instead, perhaps."

The next week flew by for Katrina. The weather was fine, but not too hot, and she and Emily walked every day, taking their packed lunch with them. Katrina was amazed at Emily's fitness. At first she had quite a job keeping up with the little lady.

"You put me to shame, Emily," she exclaimed, panting as they reached the top of a rather steep cliff path. "I thought I was fit, but you are amazing. Do you live on spinach?"

Emily laughed. "I hate spinach, as a matter of fact, but I must say I do enjoy my food. Speaking of which, what about stopping here for our picnic."

"Good idea," agreed Katrina and sat down, thankfully, on the grass.

As the days went by she found the going easier, and thoroughly enjoyed herself. Emily knew some wonderful walks and all the doubts Katrina had had about spending her holiday with this sprightly old lady faded fast. They talked a lot, as they walked, about all sorts of subjects as well as personal things. Emily had travelled widely with her husband and knew much more about the world than Katrina.

As they were having a nightcap in the bar, on Katrina's last evening, she said, "Thank you for giving me such a wonderful holiday Emily. It's been such fun. You will keep in touch won't you?"

"Of course. Thank you for being such a great companion. I do hope you manage to see Charles again before he goes off to America. It would be sad if he went off without sorting out your differences."

"Yes, you're right. Maybe he'll be home again when I get back and we can sort something out."

During one of their walks Katrina had told Emily all about Charles and the American trip and Emily had been very understanding. It had been like a kind of therapy, going over the whole story with her, and at the same time getting things sorted in her own mind. Emily had agreed that big cities could be very lonely, making Katrina feel better about her decision.

Next morning Katrina set off for home. She was really sad to leave the hotel and Emily. It had been one of the best holidays she had ever had. It was a much nicer drive home. The weather was fine for a start, and she felt refreshed after her trip and fit for anything. The miles flew by.

The next day Sue phoned.

"Did you have a good time?" she enquired.

"Marvellous thanks. I'll tell you all the details on Friday, but suffice to say I have walked the length and breadth of Cornwall with the sweetest little old lady you have ever met."

"Fascinating," replied Sue sarcastically. "I can't wait to hear the details. Now, the reason I've phoned is that I have had Charles here, looking very hangdog and sorry for himself. He wanted to know where you were. I told him you were having a holiday and that I didn't know your address, but that you would be back today. I hope that was alright."

"Thanks Sue. Is he back at home now?"

"Oh, yes. Darren went over on Sunday and did the garden with him. He told Darren that he was going to America and asked him to carry on while he was away. He said to ask you if he had any problems about what to do. I gather Charles is going to go on paying him for three hours a week, though obviously Darren didn't say that the money was going to you."

"It's a bit of a cheek telling Darren to speak to me without asking me first, but never mind. Perhaps he'll ask later. Did he tell you or Darren when he was going?"

"Next week I think he said, but I don't know which day."

"OK, thanks Sue. See you on Friday, when I shall bore you with my tales of walking in Cornwall."

Sue laughed. "I am so excited I can hardly wait," she mocked. "Bye, Katrina."

Katrina sat and stared into space wondering what to do about Charles. Should she phone him at work or let him make the first move? Eventually she decided on the later and went back to her housework.

That evening she was on tenterhooks, expecting Charles at any moment, but he didn't come. Perhaps she should have phoned him at work to say that she was home. At last she gave up waiting and went to bed to spend a fitful night arguing with herself.

By the following evening she had convinced herself that she was not going to see Charles before he left for America. The whole affair was over as quickly as it had begun. Put it down to experience, she told herself. Then the doorbell rang. She got up to answer it very slowly, hoping it was not just somebody wanting to sell her double glazing. She needn't have worried. There stood Charles on the doorstep holding an enormous bunch of flowers and looking very apologetic and wary.

"Am I forgiven?" he asked, holding out the flowers for her. Although she had been quite ready to be very cool and aloof with him, as soon as she saw him standing there she melted and couldn't stop a large smile spreading across her face.

She took the flowers from him and said, "Thank you, they're beautiful. Come in, we have a lot to talk about." He followed her into the sitting room.

"Would you like a drink?" she enquired.

"Yes, that would be nice. A whisky perhaps."

Katrina fetched the drinks and they sat down together on the big chairs.

"You look wonderful Katrina. I hear you have been to Cornwall. Did you have a good time?"

84

"Marvellous, thank you." She told him about Emily and the walking and the hotel, while he sat back listening and sipping his drink. Finally she said, "Enough about me, what have you been up to? When are you off?"

"I've been staying in London for a few days, sorting things out ready for my trip." Katrina noticed that he looked a bit embarrassed when he mentioned London. "I leave next Tuesday. Would you be able to take me to the airport?"

"Yes, of course." They sat for a while in silence. Katrina wanted to know who he stayed with in London, but wasn't sure if she dare ask. There was a definite tension in the room and the only way to break it was to ask.

"Did you stay with Sonja in London?" she asked bravely.

There was a minute's silence, while Charles toyed with the idea of lying.

"Yes, I did actually," he admitted. "I'm sorry, Katrina, I behaved like a jerk. I was so devastated that you didn't want to come to New York with me. I was so sure that you would be thrilled with the idea. When you said no, I just felt I had to get away and I knew Sonja would put me up. She was delighted that we had had a tiff and kept saying that she could see you weren't right for me when she saw you in the park that day. In the end I got fed up with her crowing, came to my senses and came back home. By this time you had gone off on your travels and I couldn't even talk to you and apologise. Oh Katrina, I have missed you. You haven't changed your mind about coming with me, have you?"

"No, sorry Charles. Though I know I shall miss you an awful lot. Will you phone me and write me nice letters?"

"Of course. I shall write and tell you about all the wonderful things you are missing and in the end you will wish you had changed your mind, you see."

Katrina laughed and wondered to herself if he might not be right.

Charles and Katrina saw each other every evening after that, knowing that these were the last few days they would have together for the next six months. Tuesday arrived too soon and Katrina drove Charles to the airport to catch his plane for the States feeling on the brink of tears but trying to be brave. As she stood on the roof and watched his plane take off for New York, she felt the tears spill over at last. She was going to miss him terribly.

Spring turned into summer and the shop was full of bright cotton dresses. Charles rang frequently and, as promised, tried to make her jealous of the high life he was leading. She laughed it off and counted the days till his return.

Darren went to court again and was let off with a caution, thanks mainly to his boss at Tescos, who gave him a very good character reference. He was also promoted to the checkout and was very proud of himself. His disco business was slowly building up a reputation and he and Chris had gigs most Saturdays. He still did Charles's garden every Sunday, and his debt to Katrina was nearly paid off. At last Sue could stop worrying about him. She was still going out regularly with Patrick, and Katrina missed their suppers together at the Bistro, though she was pleased to see her friend so happy.

One evening in July Katrina got a phone call from Emily. They had kept in touch by letter since their holiday together, but this was the first time Emily had phoned.

"How are things?" she asked Katrina.

"Rather awful at the moment actually. I miss Charles terribly and my friend Sue is out with her boyfriend more and more and I am feeling rather lonesome."

"Never mind. Tell you what, why don't I come over and stay for a few days and cheer you up?"

"Oh Emily, that would be marvellous. When can you come?"

"How about next Tuesday?"

"That would be fine," replied Katrina, suddenly feeling much better. "Shall I send you a map and directions?"

"Yes, please. I'll be with you for tea. See you then, Bye"

Katrina was thrilled that Emily was coming to stay. They had had such a good time in Cornwall.

She began to plan outings that she felt Emily would enjoy and hoped that the fine weather would hold.

However, when Emily arrived the following Tuesday, Katrina was shocked by her appearance. She had changed from a fit seventy year old to a little old woman. Katrina guessed that she had lost a lot of weight and she seemed to have lost some of her old bounce. She also had a very nasty cough. However, her wonderful smile was still there as Katrina welcomed her and took her into the house. She hoped that Emily would tell her what the problem was later, but now it was time for tea and making plans for tomorrow.

The two friends talked late into the evening until Katrina began to notice how tired Emily was looking, and suggested bed. Next day they had planned to get up early and walk round the park before having lunch in the local pub.

"I'm afraid its not as beautiful here as Cornwall, but it's a lovely park and I think you will enjoy it."

"I'm sure I will. Good night, Katrina, and thank you for that lovely meal."

Next morning Katrina was up early as planned. There was no sign of Emily so she decided to take her up some tea. She knocked on the bedroom door, but there was no reply, so she went in carrying the cup. Emily was lying very still and white, her head resting on her blood stained pillow. Katrina gave a little cry. She had heard Emily coughing in the night and wished now that she had got up and gone to check the little lady. She felt for Emily's pulse, but could find nothing. A terrible fear gripped Katrina. She felt her friends hand and it was ice cold. Katrina ran downstairs and phoned the doctor. After a bit of a tussle with the receptionist she eventually got through.

"Hello, Dr Adams. Sorry to bother you. This is Katrina Blackmore. I have a friend staying with me and I have just taken her a cup of tea. I think she's dead. Could you come round, please?"

"Of course, Katrina. What makes you think she is dead? Has she been ill?"

"She's ice cold and white as a sheet and there is blood on her pillow. Please come, I don't know what to do."

"All right, I'll come as quickly as I can."

Katrina sat in the sitting room staring into space. She jumped when the doorbell rang and ran to answer it. She was pleased it was Dr Adams on the doorstep. He had looked after her family for years and had been particularly kind to her through the divorce. She felt he was a friend. She took him upstairs to see Emily. He examined her gently then took Katrina downstairs again. They sat in the sitting room and Dr Adams gently explained what would happen next.

"I'm afraid I shall have to notify the police about your friend. You see, I can't sign a death certificate as I have never seen her before, there will have to be a post mortem. First of all can you give me her name and address."

Katrina hated the idea of poor Emily being examined, but she realised that was the law so, without protest, she gave Dr Adams the details he wanted and he went off to phone the police. When he had finished he sat down again with Katrina.

"Now, can you tell me all you know about Mrs Mills. How long have you known her, did you know she was ill and so on. I shall leave a note for the police when they come and I'd like to have all the details correct."

Katrina told Dr Adams all she knew and he wrote it all down, along with his finding when he examined Emily.

When he had finished he said, "Now Katrina, will you be alright if I leave you now? Is there anything else I can do for you? This must have been a horrible shock for you."

"No, I'll be fine. Thank you for coming so quickly. Can I get you a coffee or anything before you go?"

"No, thank you. Much as I would love to sit here and talk, I think I had better get on. Let me know if there is anything else I can do, won't you?"

"Of course." She showed the doctor out and went back to the sitting room to wait for the police. She felt amazingly calm and in control. Somehow Emily's death was so awful, her brain had gone into deep denial. She felt as if she was working on a kind of automatic pilot. A constable arrived at last, a young serious looking man with a large notebook. He too turned down a cup of coffee and they sat together as he asked Katrina his questions.

"Don't think of me as a policeman," he began, "but as an agent for the coroner. Now, perhaps you could tell me exactly what happened." Katrina went through the story again while the policeman made notes. He read the letter from Dr Adams and asked Katrina which funeral director she wished to deal with. Katrina knew no names, so left it to the policeman to recommend one. He did so, then phoned them to collect Emily's body as soon as possible. The policeman asked to see Emily before he left, so Katrina took him upstairs and left him to it. She went into the kitchen and made herself a strong cup of coffee. The events of the morning were beginning to take their toll and she could feel a headache coming on. She heard the policeman come down the stairs and went to let him out, just as the funeral director and his assistant arrived with their big waggon. The three men spoke for a while in the driveway. Katrina went back into the house, leaving the door open, and sat drinking her coffee until the men were ready to speak to her. At last they came in, shutting the door behind them.

"Good morning Mrs Blackwell," said the older of the two men. "Roy Hammond is the name, how do you do?" Katrina shook his outstretched hand. "My deep condolences for your loss," he continued as they all sat down. "Now just a few more questions I'm afraid. I gather the name of the deceased is Mrs Emily Mills is that correct?" Katrina nodded. "Will you be wanting a local burial service or a cremation? I gather the lady lived some distance away."

Katrina thought for a moment. She wished she had someone else to talk to about this. After a few moments she said, "I have a problem. I have only known Emily, Mrs Mills, a few months and we certainly never talked about death at all. As far as I know she had no close relatives, her husband is dead and she had no children. I don't know what to do. I think she would like to be buried with her husband, but I don't even know where that is exactly."

"Ah, I see," said Mr Hammond thoughtfully. "Perhaps you could find out who her solicitor is and speak to him. Do you think you could manage that? The deceased will have to go to the hospital for the postmortem first anyway, but that shouldn't take too long. We can then keep her for you until you have decided what you want to do. On the other hand you could wash your hands of the whole thing and leave it to the authorities, if you prefer."

"Oh no," cried Katrina firmly. "She was a good friend, although I didn't know her for long. The least I can do is see to her funeral."

"Fine. I just didn't want you to feel that you had to be responsible if you didn't want to. I will wait for your further instructions."

"Thank you. You have been most kind."

"Now, perhaps you could show us where Mrs Mills is and we will take her to the hospital."

When they had gone Katrina sat down again and wondered what to do next. She felt as if she was living through some kind of dream. She wished she could wake up. She phoned Penny and told her what had happened. She arranged to go and stay with her daughter for a few days and try and sort things out. James was most helpful and found a list of solicitors in Emily's area. She spent a busy morning ringing them all up. At last she found Emily's solicitor, a Mr Constable, who was shocked and upset to hear the news and arranged to see Katrina the following day. Penny boarded out the children with a friend and drove her mother down.

Mr Constable turned out to be a short stout man, in his late fifties, Katrina guessed. She sat in his office and told him what had happened and her problem with the funeral arrangements. He listened attentively and when she had finished said, "I'm so sorry you have had such a nasty experience. However I think you are right about Emily wanting to be buried with her husband. They were very close. As far as I know she had no other relatives alive, so there is no one to write to, though I think a notice in the paper might be a good idea."

"Oh I've already done that," replied Katrina.

"Fine. Now, the expenses for the funeral can be paid out of Emily's estate, if you wish. Did you know that she left you all her money?"

Katrina was shocked. She sat back in her chair and stared at Mr Constable in amazement. He smiled and continued, "Obviously not. Sorry. I didn't mean to shock you. It's not an amazing amount I'm afraid, but it will easily cover the funeral expenses, and if you sell the house that should bring in quite a lot."

Katrina left the office in a daze and went to meet Penny. They sat in a cafe with a large pot of tea and a sandwich, while Katrina told her what Mr Constable had said. Penny was equally amazed at the turn of events.

"I don't know where to start," exclaimed her mother. "I have a funeral to arrange, a GP to see, a house to sell. Shall we go and see it when we've had this tea? Mr Constable has given me the address."

"Yes, let's," replied Penny with enthusiasm. "You know how much I enjoy looking at other peoples houses." They laughed.

When they had finished their tea they went and bought a map of the area and drove to Emily's house. It turned out to be a pretty little cottage, set back from the road and surrounded by a beautiful garden. Katrina had been given the key by the police when they had checked Emily's effects, so Penny parked the car and they went up the drive to the cottage.

"This is very strange," remarked Katrina putting the key in the door. "I feel we're intruding."

"Well, according to the solicitor it's your house now, so you shouldn't feel bad."

"I suppose so. It still feels strange."

They went in and looked round. Unlike Mr Pan's house, it was as neat as a pin. The furniture was gleaming and there was a wonderful smell of polish in the air. All the rooms were small but nicely furnished and there were ornaments everywhere, souvenirs of countries Emily had been to with her husband, Katrina suspected.

"What a lovely home," Penny exclaimed. "I do wish I had met Emily."

Katrina suddenly sat down and began to weep. The house was so full of Emily's ghost. Penny put an arm around her and tried to comfort her.

"It's so silly," protested Katrina through her tears. "I only knew Emily for such a short time and I feel as if I have lost an old friend. She was such a wonderful old lady."

"Cheer up, Mum. At least she died happy, looking forward to her holiday with you. It was nice for her to go so quickly like that, but obviously not very nice for you."

91

Katrina blew her nose and wiped her eyes. "I suppose you're right. Now, I must pull myself together. I have to find the name of her GP and talk to him. Lets see if we can find an address book somewhere."

Mother and daughter searched and eventually found the doctors number in Emily's address book. Katrina got through but he was out.

"Let's go home again now, shall we?" suggested Penny. "I know there's lots more to be done, but nothing that can't wait and you look exhausted."

Her mother agreed that she had had enough for one day, so they locked up the little cottage and drove home, taking Emily's phone numbers with them.

Next day, Katrina phoned Emily's GP and told him everything that had happened. He had in fact already been notified by the police and had talked to the coroner, but he was very pleased to hear from Katrina anyway. She asked him if Emily had been ill and he confirmed it.

"She had an inoperable cancer of the lung but refused to let that interfere with her life. She knew she hadn't long to live, but she was going to make the most of what she had. She seemed to be very fond of you and spoke about you a lot. I think the holiday you both had in Cornwall did her the world of good. She was so devastated when her husband died."

"Do you know if she has any relatives at all? I'm making arrangements for the funeral, but I don't want to upset anyone by not asking them. The other thing is, do you know where her husband is buried?"

"I don't know of any relatives; no one she was in touch with anyway. Her husband is buried at St Peters, here in the village. Do you want the telephone number of the vicar there?"

"Yes, please," she said gratefully. "Thank you so much for all your help."

She took down the number of the vicar and rang off.

Two weeks later Katrina stood by Emily's newly filled grave and let the tears pour down her face. It had been a moving service and she was pleased that the little church was quite full of friends and neighbours. She had been afraid that only Penny and herself would be there. It was strange that there were no relatives. Katrina had put the time and date of the funeral in several papers, but no one had come forward. Penny took her Mother's arm and led her back to the car.

"Let's go and find some lunch," she suggested." I spotted a lovely looking pub in the village."

"I don't feel hungry," replied Katrina. "However, perhaps I shall feel better for a bit of nourishment."

"I'm sure you will," agreed her daughter.

As they sat eating their meal in the pub Penny had spotted, Katrina got the distinct impression that they were being stared at by the local inhabitants. It made her feel very uncomfortable and she was glad when the meal was over and they could leave.

"That was spooky," she said as they got back in the car. "Did you feel everyone was staring at us? Do you think that they resented the fact that I arranged the funeral without consulting the locals?"

"No, I think they were just curious," replied Penny reassuringly.

"You're probably right. I expect I'm just being paranoid, but I did feel a sense of antagonism in that pub. I shall be glad to be home again anyway. Thank you so much for coming with me today, Penny. I'm afraid I have taken you away from your family rather a lot lately. Anyway, now the funeral is over things can get back to normal again."

"Don't worry, Mum, I was pleased to help. Let's hope the house sells quickly, then you won't have that to worry about and you'll be rich."

"Yes, strange how things turned out isn't it? I still can't believe that Emily left me everything. But no one has come forward to contest the will so I suppose the money must be mine."

"Have you any plans for spending it?"

"No, not as yet, but it will be nice to think it's there if I need it. However I shall have to sell the house first. It could take ages."

CHAPTER SIX

In September, after many false alarms and a slight drop in the asking price, Emily's house sold. Katrina breathed a sigh of relief when the agent phoned her to tell her the news. She had been worried that if it hadn't sold by the autumn, it could stay on the market till the spring, when the market usually picked up again. She had driven down, from time to time, to see to the house clearance and check everything was all right with the property all through the summer, but she dreaded having to do the long trip all through the winter. She still got a spooky feeling about the village and was always pleased to leave. No one ever spoke to her, and she wondered how Emily had coped, after her husband had died, in such a tight little community. Perhaps she had lived there long enough to belong and they had all rallied round to look after her. There were certainly a lot of people at the funeral.

One evening, as Katrina was doing a bit of weeding and tidying up the garden, she had an unexpected visit from Sue.

"Sorry to bother you," she said as Katrina led her into the kitchen to put the kettle on.

"No trouble," insisted Katrina, noting that her friend looked as if she hadn't slept lately. Her first thought was that Darren had been up to no good again. They went into the sitting room with their tea and Sue sank back into her chair and took a deep breath.

"Now, what on earth is the matter?" asked Katrina. "If you will excuse me saying so, you look awful."

"I must say, I feel pretty foul," she replied and burst into tears. Katrina went across and put her arms round her friend to comfort her. When at last Sue managed to pull herself together she continued,

"It's so awful I don't know where to begin," she blew her nose and started again.

"Patrick has left me. Before he went he persuaded me to invest in some company or other that had been highly recommended to him. Instead of checking it out, I just blindly gave him the money. You met him, you know what a charmer he could be. It never crossed my mind that this could be a con. I've been so stupid, and now I don't know what to do." She looked up at Katrina with such a look of desolation on her face that Katrina dare not tell her friend that she had always suspected that Patrick was too charming to be true.

Instead she said,"Now let me get this straight. You have given Patrick a lot of money for shares and he has run off with it, is that about the gist of it?"

"Yes," agreed Sue, twisting her sodden handkerchief round her fingers. "That's the situation in a nutshell. According to Patrick, I should be receiving big dividends on my investment by now, instead of which I'm almost broke, with a hundred bills that need paying and nothing to pay them with. I'm at my wits end. I know it's an almighty cheek, but could you possibly lend me some money, just to tide me over? If I don't get some soon I'm going to lose the business."

Katrina sat back in her chair and thought things through. She certainly had the money to help her friend out but was it a wise thing to do? Would lending Sue large sums of money spoil their friendship?

"Have you tried the bank?" she asked. "I don't want to be mean about this but I can see problems if I am working for you when you owe me money."

"I already have a big mortgage with the bank and I don't think they will lend me any more. With their interest rates I probably couldn't afford to pay them back anyway."

"I see." There was a silence while Katrina tried to think of a plan. "Perhaps the answer is for me to buy into the shop," she suggested at last. "Say a third share or something like that. My son in law is a solicitor, and I'm sure he could help us work something out. Instead of paying me wages you could give me a percentage of the profits. As time goes by, if you want to, you could buy me out. Meanwhile you would have some cash to pay the bills. What do you think?"

Sue's face brightened. "Oh Katrina, what an amazing idea. Do you think it could be arranged? I don't know what I would do if I had to sell the shop, I would hate to have to work for someone else again. Oh God, I feel so stupid, getting myself in such a mess."

"Don't blame yourself too much, Sue. Good con artists are pretty hard to spot. After all, that's how they make their living. Now let me take you out to supper to celebrate our new business, you look as if you could do with a bit of looking after, and I've missed our meals at the Bistro."

"I'm sorry I've neglected you so much lately," exclaimed Sue. "Supper at the Bistro sounds great. Thank you so much for being such a wonderful friend. Can I use your bathroom and tidy myself up a bit? I feel a real wreck."

They both went upstairs to tidy up. Katrina felt rather pleased with herself. She hoped James would agree with her plan and be able to draw up the necessary papers. It seemed the perfect answer.

Two days later Katrina went to see James at his office. They both felt it would be better to keep the whole thing on a very official basis. She was shown into James's office by his secretary. She almost expected James to get up from his desk and shake hands, it was very strange.

"Morning, Katrina," he said spoiling the formality straight away.

"Shouldn't that be Mrs Blackwell?" she teased, sitting down.

"No, I think that's taking things too far," James replied laughing. "Now I believe you have a financial deal you wish to discuss with me."

"That's right," she replied and told him of Sue's problems and her idea for helping her out. When she had finished she asked, "What do you think? Would my idea work?"

"I can't see why not. What would happen if there are no profits from the company, could you manage all right without your income from the shop?"

"Oh yes. Peter is still paying me maintenance and I will probably have some of Emily's money left in the bank. It shouldn't be a problem."

"Fine. As long as you realise that if Sue gets into financial problems again you may loose all your money."

"I don't think she will. On the whole the shop is doing pretty well. Sue just has a bit of a cash flow problem at the moment. I'm sure it will sort itself out."

"Well, I'm glad you are so optimistic. I don't think there are any other problems I can think of. I'll get the papers drawn up, then you and Sue can come in and sign them. I will have to check with the bank to see that the company is viable but hopefully that will just be a formality."

"Thanks so much, James. I'll wait to hear from you then."

Katrina left the office feeling rather excited that she was soon to have a share in the little dress shop. She was quite sure that it would be a good investment in the long run. Sue was very pleased to hear that James had thought it would be a viable arrangement and was quite unperturbed that he would have to contact her bank. When Katrina spoke to Charles about the arrangement he was less than enthusiastic.

"Are you sure it's a good idea?" he enquired. "That family always seems to be in trouble, first Darren, now Sue. I hope she isn't taking advantage of your kind heart."

"Don't worry. James is going to check it all out with the bank and make sure the agreement is watertight. I think he thought I was being a bit foolhardy too."

"All I can say is that it's a good thing I shall be home again in about a month, then I can look after you. You have certainly lived an exciting life while I have been away."

Katrina laughed. "Have you got a date yet, for your return trip, I mean? I can't wait to see you again."

"No. It's a bit vague at the moment. Depends on Phil's state of health, basically. Apparently he's longing to get back so it shouldn't be long now."

When at last Charles rang off Katrina sat for a long time thinking about their relationship. She wondered if he would ask her to marry him again, and if so would she say 'yes' this time? She had missed him terribly, but did she really want the commitment of marriage? And what about Sonja? Would he still see her if they were married? She would just have to play it by ear when Charles got back. It was no good worrying about it now. She got up and went to make herself some supper.

Next morning, being Friday, Katrina got up early and drove into work. She parked her car and walked to the shop. It was a lovely sunny morning and she felt on top of the world. Sue was settling down to life without Patrick, Charles would soon be home and all was well in her world. The sight that greeted her as she turned the corner to the shop made her stop dead in her tracks, and brought her down to earth again with a bump. The space where the little boutique had stood was a smouldering wreck, steaming in the morning light. Two fire engines and a police car were parked in the road and there were groups of people standing round deep in conversation. Katrina could hardly believe her eyes. She searched the crowd for Sue, spotting her at last talking to one of the firemen. She walked across.

"What on earth has happened?" she enquired as Sue turned and saw her.

"Oh, Katrina, thank goodness you're here. They think that someone has burnt the shop down deliberately. They found some petrol cans. Everything's gone. The shop, the clothes, everything."

She put her arm around Katrina and sobbed onto her shoulder. Katrina did her best to comfort her friend, noticing suddenly that Sue had a very nasty bruise coming up on her cheek. She wondered where that had come from. The fireman she had been speaking to asked, "I gather you are a friend of Mrs. Cooper?"

"Yes," replied Katrina. "I work for her in the shop. Has anyone any idea who could have done this awful thing?"

"No, I'm afraid not as yet. I was going to ask you if you could cast any light on the matter. Do you know of anyone who might have had a grudge against Mrs Cooper?"

"Sorry," said Katrina, thinking for a moment of Patrick, then dismissing the idea. What would he have to gain after all? "Couldn't it just be an arsonist getting a kick, do you think?"

"Possibly, but I get a feeling that there is more to it than that. Anyway perhaps you could take Mrs Cooper home now. The police and I have asked her all the relevant questions for the moment, but we may need some more information as time goes by.

Could I have your name and address in case we need to contact you."

Katrina obliged and then drove Sue home to her house. She made them both some strong coffee and asked Sue to tell her exactly what had happened.

Sue gulped down a mouthful of coffee and began."The police phoned me about six o'clock this morning and said that the shop was on fire and could I go down there at once. It was awful seeing everything going up in flames like that. I shall never forget it as long as I live."

"To be practical for a moment, have you phoned your insurance company?"

"Yes, thanks, I did it on the mobile while I was waiting to talk to the police. They are sending someone down to assess the damage."

"Fine. Now what about Darren? He's going to get an awful shock if he goes to see you in the shop and it's just a burnt out shell."

"Oh yes. I woke him before I went off this morning. He'll be at work now, but he may phone or come round when he's finished."

"Fine. Now how about going upstairs and trying to get some sleep. You look exhausted and where did you get that horrible bruise on your face?"

Sue touched the bruise and winced, it was obviously very painful. "Ah yes, the bruise. The police wanted to know about that. I told them I had hit it on a cupboard door. I don't think they believed me. Perhaps I should tell you the truth though. I think I know who the arsonist is."

Katrina could hardly believe her ears. "What are you talking about? Who on earth would want to burn down the shop?" she enquired in amazement.

"I didn't say anything to the police, because I could be quite wrong, but this is what happened. Last night I had a visit from my ex husband Sam. I hadn't seen or heard from him for five years then suddenly there he was on the door step. I really wasn't at all pleased to see him as you can imagine. At first he was very charming, asking how I was and what Darren was up to. For a moment I thought perhaps he had changed and really cared how we were getting on, but no. In the end it all came out. He needed money to pay some gambling debts and had somehow heard I was doing well with the shop and thought I was good for a loan 'for old times sake.'

"I was almost honest with him and told him I had recently lost a lot of money on duff shares and couldn't loan him anything at the moment. I didn't tell him about your money of course. Anyway, he didn't believe me and thought I was just being tight fisted. That's when he started beating me up, and that's when I got my bruise. I was really terrified. I thought he was going to kill me. He always had a bad temper. Thank the Lord Darren decided to choose that moment to return from the pub. If he hadn't, I dread to think what would have happened. Darren dragged him away from me and threatened him with the police if he didn't go away and never come back. I think Sam was quite amazed at how big Darren is now, after all, he hadn't seen him for five years. Anyway he went off and that's the last we saw of him. Sam is not a good looser and I wouldn't put it past him to go off and think of a way to get his revenge, setting fire to the shop probably seemed the perfect answer."

"Don't you think it would be wise to tell the police all this?" asked Katrina, still trying to take in what Sue had said.

"No, after all, I've no proof that Sam was involved. I think I would rather the police thought it was just a stray arsonist and left it at that. If Sam comes back, however, I may think again."

"Do you think he will?"

"I doubt it. I think he was rather scared of Darren and he doesn't know what I have told the police. Anyway I thought you should know the position."

"Thanks, Sue. Now how about going up for that nap? I'll wake you if anything happens."

Sue went up to bed, leaving Katrina to think about the morning's events. She was unhappy about not telling the police about Sam but perhaps Sue knew best.

Early in the afternoon Darren arrived, starving hungry after his long mornings work at Tescos. Sue was still asleep, so Katrina made the two of them some lunch and took the opportunity to talk to him about his thoughts on recent events.

"Do you think that your father started the fire?" she asked, as they ate their sandwiches.

"I really don't know, but he was pretty mad when he left the house. I wouldn't put it past him."

"Well, your Mother has decided not to tell the police about her suspicions so I suppose we had better forget about it. I just hope they don't find out it was him, because Sue might be in trouble if they do. She has withheld information in a way."

"I think my father will be long gone by now. He has some rather nasty creditors chasing him, by all accounts, so he'll be wanting to keep a low profile."

It amazed Katrina that neither Sue nor Darren seemed too worried about what happened to Sam. They had obviously both been badly hurt by him when he left them in the lurch.

"Well, enough about the fire for the moment," said Katrina changing the subject. "What have you been up to lately?"

"Well, the job is going well and the disco business seems to be taking off. Luckily Chris knows a lot of people who need music for parties and I think our fee is pretty reasonable, which helps. Chris is taking a gap year at the moment, before he goes to University, and is planning to do some travelling after Christmas. I don't know what I shall do then. I suppose I could manage by myself, we shall see."

"Couldn't Tracey help you? It would be sad to give up the business just as it is getting going."

"She's not very keen. Anyway we may not have any work by then."

Just then Sue came down to join them, looking a lot better after her sleep. Katrina made her a snack and took it into the sitting room, just as Darren was saying goodbye. The two friends were left alone and spent the afternoon discussing how they would like the shop to be rebuilt. Sue drew lots of plans on bits of paper, while Katrina made suggestions.

"The problem is we can't do anything till the insurance money comes through. Then we need an architect and planning permission. It's going to take such a long time. What are we going to do with ourselves?" moaned Sue.

"When the police give us permission I suppose we could start clearing up the mess a bit," suggested Katrina.

"I suppose we could. Have you got some good overalls?" laughed Sue.

As it turned out, Sue engaged professionals to clear up. The fire inspector had said it was much too dangerous for amateurs. Katrina and Sue were very relieved that they had an excuse not to do the work. The money came through from the insurance and Sue found an architect, and spent long hours discussing with him what she wanted in the new shop. Katrina helped order new stock and furnishings. It was rather exciting starting from scratch.

At the beginning of November Charles came home from America. Katrina went up to Heathrow to meet him from the plane. She could hardly contain her excitement and sang happily as she drove along. She parked the car and went into the terminal to find the correct arrival gate. Suddenly her heart missed a beat. There, standing by the barrier looking like someone dressed for the fashion pages of Vogue, stood Sonja. 'What was she doing there for goodness sake?' thought Katrina, with a sinking feeling in her stomach. At that moment Sonja spotted her and walked across to where Katrina stood rooted to the spot.

"Hello Katrina. What are you doing here?" she enquired.

"I've come to meet Charles," she stammered.

"Oh, what a pity you've had a wasted journey. Didn't Charles tell you? He's spending the night with me in London," retorted Sonja, looking down at Katrina as if she was something unpleasant.

Katrina could hardly believe her ears. She just stood and stared. Suddenly all the joy of the morning evaporated. People were beginning to come down the walkway from the plane. There was no way she was going to stand there and fight over Charles. She turned and ran from the building with tears streaming down her face. She drove home in a daze.

What on earth was going on? She had spoken to Charles last night on the phone and he had said, "See you tomorrow at the airport." Had she misheard? All these questions went round and round in her head as she drove.

At last she reached home and went straight up to bed, getting in with all her clothes on and covering her head with the duvet to block out the world. It was all too awful to cope with.

She must have dozed off because the next thing she heard was the sound of the phone ringing. She got up and went downstairs to answer it.

"Katrina? Whatever happened to you at the airport?" asked Charles from the other end of the line.

"I came to meet you, as planned, and was told by your darling Sonja that you had arranged to go home with her, so I left. There was no way I was about to have a fight over you in the middle of the terminal," Katrina answered crossly. "Now perhaps you will leave me in peace to go back to bed," and she slammed the receiver down. She went back to bed but couldn't sleep. Finally she took a pill and eventually dozed off.

Next morning Sue phoned. "Well how's Charles?" she enquired brightly.

"I don't know, and I don't care," replied Katrina savagely. She explained to Sue what had happened.

"What on earth is the silly man playing at?" demanded her friend.

"Don't ask me. Bloody men."

"I'll tell you what, why don't we go out for the day, somewhere nice? I'll be over in about an hour. You need a treat."

"Thanks, Sue. That would be great. See you in an hour." The day was cold and clear and the two friends drove out into the country and found a nice pub for lunch. It was a good basic meal and Katrina felt a lot better for it. She suddenly realised that she hadn't eaten since breakfast the day before.

As they drank their coffee Sue asked, "Now what are you going to do about Charles? It's rather bad luck that you live so close to each other. It's going to be difficult to avoid him completely."

"Yes I know. The question is, do I want to avoid him?"

"Ah well, only you can answer that."

"I was so happy setting off to meet him yesterday, then there was the dreaded Sonja to spoil it all."

"Maybe you should have let him explain himself on the phone. Never mind, it's too late now. What shall we do this afternoon? How about some shopping?"

"Yes, please. Shopping with you is such a hoot. Let's go and spend some money."

They drove to their favourite shopping centre and spent a very enjoyable afternoon trying on a lot of clothes, but buying very few. As they drove home again Katrina said, "Thank you so much for a lovely day Sue. I have really enjoyed myself. I hope I haven't kept you from work."

"No, there was nothing special I had to do today. Shall we go and see the shop on the way home?"

"Yes let's. The builders must be almost finished by now."
The men had all gone home by the time they arrived, so they let themselves in and looked round. Katrina hadn't seen the shop for a while and she was very impressed by the way it was shaping up.

"It looks so big with no fittings doesn't it?" she remarked. "We'll soon be able to get in and start decorating by the look of things."

"They reckon another week. I can't wait, I've got all the paint ready."

"Great. When do you think we will be ready to reopen?"

"I'm planning a big party here at the end of the month. That should give us enough time. I thought I would send invitations to all our regulars, what do you think?"

"Sounds good to me."

The Grand Opening was a great success. Sue and Katrina had worked very hard to get everything ready in time, cleaning, painting, sewing curtains then finally sorting out all the new stock. They had painted the walls in Apple White and all the skirting boards in a Catkin Green. The material for the curtains and changing cubicles had a cream background with a design of green leaves all over it. On the night of the opening they had served wine and nibbles to their invited guests and had received some very nice compliments on the new decor and the range of clothes, now displayed carefully on the racks. By the end of the exciting evening, the two friends felt they had done a good job and that trade would soon pick up after their ten weeks closure.

Katrina had still heard nothing from Charles. It was strange that she had spoken to him almost every day while he was in America, but now he was back in England she didn't even know where he was living. She was pleased that she had been so busy. It had kept her mind off wondering about him. Life settled back into a routine and she began to think about Christmas. She arranged to have all the family as usual and started making Christmas puddings and a cake in readiness. Mark was living with Sarah, but there was still no talk of wedding bells.

"Maybe they won't bother," suggested Penny one afternoon as she sat with her mother drinking tea. "Lots of people don't these days, you know."

"I suppose you're right but it would be nice to have a good wedding," Katrina replied.

"You're just old fashioned, Mum, that's your trouble. I thought maybe the next wedding would be yours and Charles' but that seems a bit out of the question now. Pity, really, he was nice."

Katrina suddenly felt very cross with her daughter. "I don't believe you said that," she exploded. "I'm trying to forget that wretch as a matter of fact. He behaved atrociously."

"You still miss him though don't you?"

Katrina thought for a moment. "Yes, I suppose I do in a way."

"The thing is Mum, he came to see me," said Penny waiting for the explosion from her mother.

"He what?"

"He came to see me. He asked me if I thought there was any chance of you both getting together again."

"The cheek of the man."

"I promised to sound you out. He's really upset about what happened, apparently Sonja is always pulling those kind of stunts. Although she's not married to him any more, she is still very possessive and a real schemer."

"You can say that again."

105

"Anyway, Charles wants to meet you again and try and sort things out. I said I would ask you."

Katrina sat for a long time staring into space. Did she really want to get involved with Charles again? She was just getting over him and felt very nervous about further commitment. At last Penny said, "Go on, Mum, be brave, nothing ventured nothing gained."

Katrina couldn't help laughing at her daughter's efforts on Charles's behalf. "What's in this for you?" she asked. "You seem very keen that we should make it up."

"I like Charles and I think you would be much happier with him than without him, that's all."

Deep down Katrina knew that this was true. All of a sudden all her doubts just disappeared. Life was for living and taking risks, not pussy -footing around being careful."OK, little Miss Go-between. Tell Charles I'm willing to hear his side of the story, but it had better be good."

Penny gave her Mother a big hug. "Well done, Mum. I'm sure you won't regret it. I'll speak to Charles."

Two days later Charles phoned.

"May I take you out to dinner on Saturday?" he began. "I'm longing to see you again and I would like to explain to you my side of the story."

"Thank you, Charles, that would be very nice," replied Katrina primly. "Penny has persuaded me that you should be allowed to make your case and I suppose she is right. Will you pick me up?"

"Yes. Let's say 7.30 shall we? See you then."

When Katrina told Sue she was going out to supper with Charles she was overjoyed and gave her friend a big hug.

"I'm sure you have done the right thing," she insisted. "You two were so good together, it seems a shame to break up. I'm sure you won't regret it."

"I hope not. It's all Penny's fault if I do." They laughed.

Saturday came and the shop had its usual rush of shoppers and browsers. By the time Katrina got home she felt more like going to bed than going out. However after a hot bath she felt a lot better and began to look forward to the evening. When the doorbell rang she suddenly began to feel very nervous. She hadn't seen Charles for almost seven months. Would she still feel the same way about him, had she changed? Had he changed? She opened the door. There stood Charles looking as handsome as ever and holding an enormous bunch of flowers. Her heart missed a beat. She just stood and stared. How could she have had any doubts about her feelings for this man? She was jogged from her reverie as he asked, "May I come in?" in a rather plaintive tone.

"Of course, sorry. Come in and I'll look for a vase for those wonderful flowers." She bustled off into the kitchen with Charles following behind carrying the bouquet. She dare not look at him. She felt flustered and awkward. She busily filled the vase with water and turned to take the flowers from Charles but he had put them on the counter. He took her head in his hand and drew her to him, kissing her hungrily on the lips. Katrina felt a shiver pass through her body as she surrendered to his embrace.

"Oh, Katrina, I have missed you so much. Am I forgiven?" he mumbled into her hair.

Katrina clung to him and felt tears welling up in her eyes, all her resolve to be cool and aloof disappearing into the air. She broke away at last and stood back looking at him, tears still coursing down her cheeks.

"How could I have thought of having nothing more to do with you? I must have been mad. It's so wonderful to see you again. I feel so happy." She clung to him again and breathed in the smell of him that had always excited her so much. How could she have forgotten?

The doorbell rang and made her jump.

"Don't answer it, Katrina. Pretend we're out."

"I can't do that," she said breaking away from him. "It might be something important."

Charles sighed and let her go. On the doorstep stood two men, both strangers. Katrina wished she had taken Charles's advice.

"Good evening Madam," said the first man. "Sorry to bother you so late. I am D.I. Jones and this is Sergeant Rogers." They showed her their identity badges. "May we come in for a quick word please?"

Why did Katrina always think of Darren when she was asked for a few words by the police?

"Yes, of course. Come through," she said opening the door wider. They all trooped into the sitting room, where Charles sat browsing through a magazine.

"Evening, Sir," said D.I. Jones, obviously rather startled at finding someone else in the house.

"Evening Inspector. Should I go in the other room, Katrina?"

"No, I'm sure it won't matter if you stay. Now, gentlemen, what can I do for you?"

"I just need to ask you a few questions with regard to the fire at Mrs. Coopers shop," began the officer.

Katrina's heart sank. She thought all that was behind her now, after all, the police had said that they thought the fire had been started by an unknown arsonist.

D.I. Jones continued, "As far as you know was Mrs Cooper having financial troubles at the time of the fire?"

Katrina thought for a moment then replied, "In the middle of September, it is true that Mrs Cooper was having a few money problems. However, as I have recently come into a small legacy I was able to help her out. In fact I bought a part share of the shop, so that she would have money to cover her debts. The fire occurred about a week after my money went into her bank, so in fact she was quite solvent when it occurred."

"I see, Madam, thank you for being so frank. Just one more thing, have you any proof of the transaction?"

"Yes, of course, but why can't you ask Mrs Cooper all these questions?"

"This morning Mr Cooper was arrested for causing a shop fire in Birmingham. We believe that he is involved in an insurance scam. While he was being interviewed he mentioned that he had started the fire here and that that was also an insurance scam, on behalf of Mrs Cooper."

Katrina could hardly believe her ears. She went to her desk and found the relevant papers and showed them to the inspector.

"There," she said pointing to the date. "Proof that Mrs Cooper had no need to burn down her shop."

Katrina was very cross. The inspector looked carefully at the document and made a few notes then passed it back to Katrina. "Thank you for your cooperation, Madam. Well, I think that will be all for now," he said getting up and moving towards the door. Katrina showed the two policemen out and returned to Charles.

"What on earth was all that about?" he enquired.

She explained to him about Sue's suspicions that her exhusband had started the fire for spite. Now he was trying to get her into trouble with the police, suggesting an insurance scam.

"Should I phone Sue, do you think?"

"I should keep right out of it if I was you. You have told the police all you know and that's all you can do for the moment."

"I suppose you're right," sighed Katrina hoping Sue would be all right.

"Now, how about supper?" suggested Charles trying to regain Katrina's attention. "I'd better ring the restaurant and check they still have our table."

Luckily the Maitre d' knew Charles well, so the table was still theirs. It was a wonderful evening and Katrina soon forgot about Sue and Sam and the fire. By the time they had finished eating a small three piece band had started to play, and people were getting up to dance on the "postage stamp" dance floor.

"May I have the pleasure of this dance?" asked Charles, rather formally.

"Certainly," replied Katrina in the same tone. "I should be delighted."

They got up laughing and made their way through the tightly packed tables. The music was soft and melodic and they danced very close together, oblivious to every one but themselves. It was magic. Katrina silently thanked her daughter for insisting that she gave Charles another chance.

Much later, as she lay in Charles's arms in her big bed she asked, "By the way what did happen at the airport?"

"Ah yes, the airport," he replied, trying to remember exactly what had happened and the best way to tell Katrina. "Well, I was met by Sonja and I asked her if she had seen you. She said you had suddenly rushed off and that I had better go home with her and get some rest after the flight. I thought that perhaps one of your family had been taken ill or something. Sonja was so vague. Then I phoned you and you were so cross, I got suspicious and made her explain exactly what had happened. I was furious with her and went and stayed with a friend till the next day. She has this strange notion that I am her property, just because I was once married to her. I think basically she is slightly mentally unstable. She runs her business superbly but otherwise she behaves like a small child. I'm sorry you were hurt."

"Never mind. Tonight has made up for everything. I must remember to thank Penny for making me see sense."

"Thank her from me too won't you?"

They lay together silently, both deep in thought until they drifted off to sleep, happy and content to be together again.

Next morning they got up late and spent a lazy day doing nothing in particular. Katrina thought that Sue might phone about Sam and the fire but she needn't have worried. Darren had paid her all the money back, so he wasn't doing the garden any more so even he didn't interrupt their peace.

"This is the life," said Charles lying back in his chair, sipping a last whisky before going home for the night.

"By the way," asked Katrina. "What are you doing for Christmas?"

"Hadn't thought about it really. I feel a kind of deja vu here don't you? Our relationship is a year old now. What a lot has happened!"

"It's amazing isn't it? Last Christmas seems years away. Anyway, will you chance my turkey one more time?"

"I'd love to. It will be great to see all your family again. Is Mark still with Sarah?"

"Oh yes. No sign of those two breaking up. I am very pleased actually, I'm fond of Sarah."

"Well, now that that is arranged, I had better get home and get myself sorted for the morning. I've got a rotten report to get written before I go to bed."

"Poor you. I hope the whisky hasn't blurred you judgment."

"I worry a lot more about thoughts of you creeping into my head," he said laughing and struggling out of his chair. Katrina walked to the door with him and they kissed good night.

"See you soon, Katrina. Thanks for a lovely weekend," said Charles letting her go at last.

"My pleasure," she replied, and watched him walk down the drive. She must remember to phone Penny tomorrow and thank her. Next morning in the shop, Sue couldn't wait to tell Katrina all about Sam getting arrested. "I was going to phone you, then I realised that Charles might be there, so I restrained myself."

"Thanks, Sue. I had a visit from the police too you know. They wanted proof that you wouldn't have asked Sam to burn down the shop for you. Luckily I had the papers handy to show them that you had my money before the fire. Well, let's hope that's an end to it. Did they ask you if you knew why Sam had done it?"

"Yes, they did actually. I just said it was probably because he hated the idea of me making a good living without him. They seemed to accept that. I said nothing about the row we had or my suspicions and they can't prove anything so hopefully that is that. Now, enough of my problems. How did the date go with Charles? Are you still speaking to Penny?"

"Yes, of course. We had a wonderful time, delicious supper, a little dancing, then home to BED."

"You shameless hussy!" Sue declared in mock horror. "Seriously though, I'm thrilled. What did he say about Sonja?"

"He said he thought that she was a bit unbalanced."

"From what I've heard he's probably right. I suppose that you have to live with the fact that she might make trouble again, if she gets the chance."

"Yes, and the fact that Charles feels responsible for her in a funny sort of way. At least I know what I am up against and will hopefully deal with it better next time."

"I'm sure you will. Well, enough of this chatter, time for work," exclaimed Sue.

"I've just thought of what to get you for Christmas," teased Katrina. "A whip to keep the staff in order."

111

CHAPTER SEVEN

Katrina lay in her bed on Christmas Eve, trying to get to sleep and thinking about the last two Christmases she had spent since Peter had left. The first one had been spoiled by Peter, who was living with Shirley by this time, turning up with presents for the family, not caring that it might upset her and spoil her day. It was strange that although they lived in the same town they had hardly met since then.

The second Christmas had been much better. She had been in her new house and Charles had come to lunch with her little family and fitted in so well, even playing with the children. Then they had spent their first night together. Goodness, had that been only a year ago? It seemed like a lifetime away. This year would be better still. Charles was almost like one of the family now and she wouldn't be so tense, worrying about him getting on with everyone. Considering he had no children of his own he got on marvellously well with Max and Josh, joining in with their games and telling them stories. It was such a shame that he would probably never be a father. She drifted off to sleep at last and dreamt about Charles arriving for Christmas dinner with a tribe of children he had forgotten to tell her about.

Next day she woke to the sound of rain beating on the window. "Bother," she thought as she got up for her bath. "Looks as if we are not going to be able to go for our afternoon walk this year."

Penny and James and the boys were the first to arrive, as usual, all looking very smart in their Christmas clothes.

"We have brought our new Christmas bikes," announced Josh when the general greetings were over. "Can we take them to the park after lunch?"

"Of course, darling, as long as this rain stops. What else did you get?"

"Grandma and grandpa Taylor got us dressing up clothes," chipped in Max. "I've got a space suit."

"Goodness me," said Katrina. "How about you Josh?"

"I have a pirate suit like Captain Hook," he replied. "Would you like to see?"

Charles arrived at that moment and the little boys greeted him with great excitement, longing to tell him all about the presents they had already received. Penny and Katrina retreated to the kitchen and left James and Charles to it.

"Max and Josh are very fond of Charles. He's so good with them," remarked Penny as she helped prepare the meal.

"I was thinking last night how sad it was he didn't have children," replied Katrina. "He was really good with Darren too, when they were doing the garden together. I used to take them cups of tea as they worked and they always seemed very happy in each other's company."

"How is the dreaded Darren these days, by the way?"

"He seems much more settled now I'm glad to say. His girlfriend Tracey has been a lot to do with that, I think. She keeps him well in control. The fate of the disco business is a bit in the balance at the moment though. His friend Chris is off to Australia after Christmas and Darren is going to have to find a new partner. It would be sad if he had to give it all up now, after working so hard on setting it up."

"Won't his girlfriend help him?"

"Apparently she's not very keen on the idea."

At that moment Mark and Sarah arrived so mother and daughter left the kitchen and went to wish them Happy Christmas.

"Welcome, welcome," said Katrina giving them both a big hug. It struck her that Sarah was looking a bit pale and wan and she hoped she wasn't ill. She served everyone with drinks and was surprised when Sarah asked for orange juice rather than the champagne cocktail she had prepared. They all drank a toast to a merry Christmas. Max and Josh also had orange juice and went round clicking everyone's glass saying "Cheers" with great gusto. Suddenly Mark said, "As we are all here together, Sarah and I have an announcement to make. We are having a baby, that is to say, Sarah is." He put his arm proudly around Sarah's shoulder as everyone started shouting at once and trying to hug the happy

113

couple. Although the little boys didn't really realise what was going on, they joined in too, thinking it was a new game.

Katrina was so happy, she thought she was going to burst. This news accounted for the orange juice and the wan look. She was pleased it was nothing more serious. The fact that no mention of a wedding had been mentioned seemed irrelevant. How times have changed she thought.

The rest of the day went by in a happy blur. Presents were opened, too much food was eaten, games were played and by afternoon, the weather had cleared so they were able to go for their usual walk in the park after all. The little boys took their bikes and had a wild time dashing around. The grown ups walked more sedately, chatting happily and catching up with each other's news. There was a stiff breeze blowing and Katrina was pleased to see a bit of colour return to Sarah's cheeks.

When they got back to the house, Mark went with his mother to the kitchen to help with tea and Katrina had a chance to talk to him alone about the baby.

"I don't want to sound old fashioned," she began hesitantly, "but are you two planning to get married at all?"

"Probably not before the child is born, but we shall see," replied Mark casually. "As you probably gathered, it was a bit unplanned, but we are still very thrilled. Trouble is poor old Sarah is being terribly sick in the mornings."

"I thought she looked a bit pale. That phase will soon pass hopefully. Do her parents know?"

"No, not as yet. We are going to lunch tomorrow to tell them. I get the feeling Sarah is rather worried about it."

"Oh dear, I hope they don't make a fuss. Sarah needs all the support she can get, especially if she's feeling a bit rough at the moment."

That evening, when everyone had gone home, and Charles and Katrina were sitting on the settee in a state of collapse, sipping their whisky, Charles said, "Well, there goes another perfect Christmas Day. Thank you, Katrina. Do you realise that this is our first anniversary?"

"Funnily enough I was thinking about that last night. What a year it has been."

"Too true," Charles agreed. They sat in silence for a while deep in thought, thinking of all that had happened. Suddenly Charles turned to face Katrina and took her hand and said, "Katrina will you marry me? I know you turned me down before but I was hoping I could make you change your mind this time."

She looked deep into his eyes collecting her thoughts, "Yes," she said feeling that this time she was ready. "I would like that."

Charles held her to him and squeezed her so tight she thought that she was going to suffocate. Finally she pulled herself free and said teasingly, "You're not being sent to America again are you?"

"No," he replied laughing. "This time I just want to live with you here. Oh Katrina, I have been wanting to ask you for so long but didn't have the courage. You have made me so happy. I so miss you when we are not together."

"Darling Charles, I do love you. What a way to end a perfect day. Lets go to bed shall we? There are so many arrangements to make but there's plenty of time. My brain won't cope with any more today."

"I've said it before and I'll say it again, you are a wanton woman Katrina Blackwell, but before you rush me off to bed I have another Christmas present for you." He delved in his pocket and produced a small box, which he handed to Katrina. She opened it and found, nestling in the blue velvet, a beautiful opal and diamond ring. With a beating heart she put it on her finger. It fitted her perfectly.

"Oh Charles, it's magnificent. Thank you."

"I'm so glad you like it. Now we are officially engaged so let's get upstairs and celebrate as only we know how," suggested Charles.

They laughed and chased each other up the stairs with new energy.

The first person Katrina told about her forthcoming marriage was Penny. She was thrilled and congratulated her Mother whole heartedly. "My goodness, everything is happening at once! First Mark and Sarah having a baby, then you and Charles getting married, whatever next?" she exclaimed.

"I was wondering if Mark and Sarah would get married too. Did they say anything to you? When I asked Mark he seemed a bit vague."

"No, not a thing. Poor Sarah wasn't looking very well was she?"

"No, I must say I noticed that. I gather she is being sick, poor thing. I hope Mark is looking after her and making allowances for her condition. You know what a whirl those two live in."

"It's no good worrying, Mum. They are quite old enough to look after themselves. Now enough about them, what about you and Charles, have you set a date yet?"

"We thought the end of February, no special reason apart from the fact that it would be nice to have a holiday somewhere hot, around that time. Also it gives us time to get things sorted out."

"Where are you going to live? You've both got such nice houses."

"To tell you the truth, that question is still under discussion. I think in the end we shall sell both houses and buy a completely new one. However, there is no rush."

"Would you like me to come with you to choose an outfit by the way? We could have a nice day out."

"Yes please. I'll give you a ring and we can sort something out. I'd better go now. I have an appointment with a man about the reception. I could do it myself really, but Charles says we have to have a proper do in a local hotel, so who am I to argue?"

"Quite right too. See you soon, Mum. Bye."

That evening Katrina phoned Mark to tell him her news. "Congratulations Mum, that's marvellous. I hope you will be very happy. I must say I do like Charles."

"Thanks, darling. Now tell me, how is Sarah? She looked so pale when you came at Christmas."

"To tell you the truth I am worried about her. She is being terribly sick at the moment. I managed to get her to the doctors this evening and he has given her a sick note for work, and told her to

116

stay in bed for a few days and drink plenty of fluids. Apparently she is getting dehydrated and losing weight. I wondered if she should give up work all together, but she's not keen and the doctor says this sickness should pass soon.

"The other problem is her parents. We went over to them on Boxing day and told them our news, thinking they would be thrilled, instead of which we got a lecture on the sin of living together unmarried, and having a child out of wedlock. It was awful. Sarah got in a terrible state as you can imagine and we had to leave early. Thank the Lord that my family are more broad minded."

Katrina was quite shocked to hear Mark's story. What good did these people think they would do with this narrow attitude.

"Mark, I am sorry. All Sarah needs now is a row with her parents when she is not feeling well. If there is anything I can do just let me know. If Sarah wants to come down here to stay and be looked after for a while she'd be very welcome."

"Thanks, Mum. I'll let you know how things go. Thanks for ringing. Love to Charles. Bye."

Katrina returned to the sitting room and told Charles about her conversation with Mark.

"I'm afraid I can't help you with maternity problems," he said. "I've had no experience."

"Do you ever wish you had?" she asked.

"Sometimes," he admitted. "However Sonja was very firm about not wanting children so I went along with that. She was a bit old to start having babies when we got married anyway. Thanks to you I shall soon have step children, could be the next best thing."

"Have you told Sonja about the wedding yet, by the way?" she said as casually as she could.

"No not yet. I suppose I had better do so at some point. Could be tricky." He sat deep in thought for a while thinking about the best way to tell Sonja with the least upset. Katrina did not envy him the task. To get his mind off Sonja she said, "I went to the County Hotel today to book the reception for the last Saturday in February, OK?"

Charles re-focused his mind on his forthcoming wedding and replied, "Sounds good. I suppose we should have some invitations printed, though we only need about half a dozen."

"I think we should do it properly then there won't be any confusion about dates and venues. We have so few guests we don't want to lose any."

"True. You're sure you don't want to ask anyone else?"

"No, quite sure thank you."

"Now where do you want to go for the honeymoon? We had better get that sorted out too."

"How about the Seychelles? I've never been there."

"OK, fine. I'll get that booked up. It will be nice to get some sun in February."

"Last but not least where are we going to live after we are man and wife? It seems silly to keep two houses going don't you think?"

"Yes, I suppose so," he said grudgingly. "Trouble is I don't want to lose my garden and you don't want to lose your house. The other problem is there is no way all our furniture will fit into either house."

"Quite. I'm sure the only solution is to sell both and start again."

"You're probably right. I'll tell you what, why don't we leave it till we get back from holiday? There's no rush is there?"

"OK, let's forget it for the moment then. I think that's everything sorted. The registry office is booked, the hotel for the reception. You will book the honeymoon. I shall get the invitations printed. Now all I need is a wedding outfit."

"I don't have to wear tails or anything, do I?" asked Charles plaintively.

"No, of course not," replied Katrina laughing. "A smart suit will do just fine."

"Good. That's a relief."

All the arrangements seemed to be going very smoothly and Katrina wondered why people made such a fuss about these things. Mind you it helped that there were so few people coming to the wedding, and they hadn't got large families to contend with. She hoped she hadn't forgotten something vital.

A few days later Mark phoned, sounding very anxious. "Sarah is in hospital," he announced, after exchanging the usual pleasantries. "I had to call the doctor yesterday because in spite of resting she was still being very sick. He decided that the only thing to do was to put her in hospital and give her intravenous fluids. They also did a scan to see everything was alright with the baby. It was, I'm glad to say. It's all been quite terrifying."

"Poor Sarah," said Katrina trying to keep calm. "How long do you think she will have to stay in?"

"No idea. Depends how well she gets on I suppose. I may have to take you up on your offer to have her to stay. I don't like the idea of her on her own in the flat while I'm at work, when she comes out."

"Of course, darling. I'd love to have her here as long as she wants. How are her parents taking all this?"

"They are being very cool. There's no way Sarah could go and stay with them. They are visiting her tomorrow so I hope they don't upset her. She's extra vulnerable at the moment as you can imagine."

"Oh dear, how sad. I won't visit at the moment, as she may be out soon, but do let me know if there is anything I can do won't you?"

"Thanks for your support, Mum, I do appreciate it. I'll ring again soon. Bye."

Katrina put the phone down and sat for a long time thinking about Mark and Sarah and the baby. When Penny was pregnant there were none of these worries. She was never sick, and even managed to go on working until a month before Josh was born. She felt so helpless but there was nothing she could do, just wait and hope. Tomorrow she would turn out the spare room ready for Sarah if she came. Looking on the bright side it would be fun to have her to stay. They could get to know each other better.

A week later Sarah arrived. Mark brought her down in the car after work. He looked worse than she did, and he admitted that he had not been sleeping well. Katrina persuaded him to stay the

119

night as well, and have a good nights sleep before returning to London. He agreed thankfully.

Sarah stayed for a fortnight in the end and Katrina thoroughly enjoyed her company. Penny came round to visit and bought with her a load of baby books that she had found. She talked with Sarah for hours, giving her the advantage of her experience. A lot of the information about scans and birth plans was quite new to Katrina, and she was glad of Penny's input. Mark came down at the weekend and was thrilled to see the improvement in Sarah. She was still feeling very tired, however and it was decided that she should stay another week.

One afternoon, as Sarah and Katrina were sitting having a cup of tea after a gentle walk round the park, Sarah said, "I don't really want this baby."

Katrina nearly choked on her tea. "I beg your pardon, what did you just say?" she asked in amazement.

"I don't really want this baby," Sarah repeated.

Katrina couldn't think what to say, everything had seemed to be going so well. Sarah was getting better fast and she and Mark had seemed so happy.

"How long have you felt this way?" she asked gently. "I thought you and Mark were so pleased about the baby."

"Mark was so thrilled when I told him I was pregnant, but I had my reservations right from the start. I tried so hard to be enthusiastic for his sake. Then I got ill and I thought I would feel better when I had stopped being sick, but it has made no difference. I just don't think I can cope." She put her head in her hands and began to weep. Katrina put her arm round her and tried to come to terms with the situation. Poor child must have been building up to making this announcement for weeks, and no one had suspected how awful she was feeling.

"Don't worry, Sarah," she said. "We'll sort something out. Does Mark know how you feel?"

Sarah's head jerked up and she turned to face Katrina, "Oh no, please don't tell him, will you?" she exclaimed in panic.

"Of course not, if you don't want me to, but don't you think he should know?"

"Not yet, please."

"Alright, I won't say anything. Now, can you explain what exactly is bothering you? Is it going through the birth or coping with the baby when it is born or what?"

"The whole thing terrifies me," she replied, bursting into tears again.

Katrina hoped that Penny, with all her books and advice, hadn't added to Sarah's terror. She could get very enthusiastic and she had had such easy pregnancies. Katrina was at a loss to decide what to do next. She felt that Mark was going to have to be told in the end, but she would keep her promise for the moment. She suddenly had an idea.

"Sarah, have you ever had anything to do with small babies?"

"No, not really. None of my close friends have had children yet so I haven't had an opportunity, really."

"Well, I've just had an idea. My friend Nancy has just become a grandmother and she looks after the baby while her daughter goes to work. Why don't I phone her and see if we could go and visit and see the baby. This may not help you at all but I think it's worth a go, don't you?"

Sarah looked unconvinced but agreed to go with Katrina, if Nancy was agreeable.

Katrina spoke to Nancy on the phone and explained the situation. She was only too happy to be of help.

"Come round tomorrow about ten," she said. "Sarah can watch me bath the little darling and maybe give him a bottle, if she feels up to it."

"Thanks, Nancy. That's really kind of you. Jane won't mind will she?"

"No, I'm sure she won't. I'll tell her the situation anyway and swear her to secrecy as far as Mark's concerned. You never know, they do bump into each other from time to time."

"Thanks. We'll see you tomorrow then, about ten. Bye"

Next morning Katrina and Sarah set off to Nancy's house. Both were rather nervous and sat silently, deep in their own thoughts. Nancy greeted them on the doorstep with the baby in her arms.

"Come in," she said. Katrina introduced her to Sarah who was looking extremely nervous. They all went upstairs to the spare room where Nancy had the pink plastic bath all ready.

"Now, Sarah," she said, as she sat down and started to remove the baby's small clothes, "can you just test the temperature of the water with your elbow, to see it's not too hot."

Sarah did as she was told but asked Katrina to check it too, just to make sure. Nancy washed the baby's face with cotton wool, then soaped him all over and popped him in the water. Sarah stood watching in fascination. She had never seen anything so small with no clothes on before.

"What is he called?" she asked.

"Timothy," replied Nancy. "I suppose he will end up being called Tim, but it's still Timothy at the moment." She removed the tiny baby from the water and began to dry him. He obviously enjoyed his bath and didn't make a sound.

"I'm very impressed with your technique," teased Katrina as she watched her friend put the tiny clothes back on Timothy.

"Handling babies is like riding a bike," replied Nancy. "It all comes back very quickly once you get going. Now Sarah would you like to hold Timothy while I go and make his bottle?"

Sarah sat down on a chair and took the little boy from Nancy. She did not look comfortable.

"Sit back a bit," suggested Nancy. "That's better. Now relax. Just let Timothy rest in your arms, that's the way."

A big smile spread across Sarah's face as she relaxed and began to feel more at home with the small bundle. Katrina thanked fate that Timothy was such a contented baby. The whole exercise could have been a disaster if he had cried all through his bath like some babies.

"OK?" asked Nancy. Sarah nodded. "Fine, I shall go and get the bottle then."

Katrina sat on the bed and watched Sarah smiling at the baby. So far so good, she thought. Her idea seemed to be working. Nancy came back with the bottle and showed Sarah how to test the

122

temperature of the milk on the back of her hand. Then she gave it to Sarah to feed Timothy. She managed very well, with a little help from Nancy. When the bottle was empty and Timothy had had a good burp, Nancy lay him in his crib for a sleep and they all went down for some coffee.

As they sat together sipping their drinks, Nancy asked, "Well, Sarah, do you feel a bit happier now about having your baby? Katrina said that you were a bit nervous because you had never had much to do with small children."

"Yes, I think I do," replied Sarah after some thought. "I just hope that mine is as good as Timothy."

They laughed. "I'm sure Katrina will give you a hand if you need it, and your mother too of course," she added as an afterthought.

Sarah almost told her about the row she had had with her parents, and then thought better of it. Instead she said, "Thank you so much for all your kindness. I really do feel a lot better having handled Timothy. You must be very proud of him."

"Yes I am. He is so good. I shall miss him when my daughter gives up work next month and takes him over full time."
That evening, when Mark phoned, Sarah was full of enthusiasm about her session with Timothy. He was thrilled to hear that she was feeling so much better, and sounding more like her old self at last. Katrina and Sarah visited Timothy once more before Mark came down for the weekend to take Sarah home. The second visit was just as successful as the first, and Katrina began to feel that everything was going to be all right after all. Sarah took Nancy an enormous bunch of flowers to thank her. Nancy was quite overwhelmed.

"Thank you, Sarah, these are beautiful! But you shouldn't have bothered. It's been a pleasure to see you. Do come again any time and let me know how you are getting on," she added kindly.

The following weekend Mark took a much happier Sarah home again to London. Sarah gave Katrina an enormous hug as she left saying, "Thank you so much for all your help and kindness. I feel so much better now than I did two weeks ago. Life seems manageable again."

"Pleased to be of help," replied Katrina grinning with pleasure. "Any time you want a break you know you are always welcome. I shall feel quite lonely next week without you." She stood in the road and waved as the little MG disappeared round the bend in the road. She went back into the house.

It was true that she would miss Sarah but at least she would see more of Charles now. He had kept very much out of the way while Sarah had been staying. He said he felt that the two women needed time to chat on their own. All the baby talk was too much for him. She was also able to concentrate on getting things ready for her wedding, now she was alone again. The first thing she did was to arrange to have a day out with Penny to look for her wedding outfit. They went up to London together and thoroughly enjoyed themselves trying on suits and hats. It took Katrina a long time to find exactly what she wanted, but at last she chose a buttermilk coloured straight dress with matching long swing coat and a big buttermilk hat with black trim. Penny approved.

"That's perfect," she said, as Katrina came out of the changing room to show her. "A very fitting colour for a second wedding I reckon."

"Are you sure the colour doesn't make me look washed out?"

"Not at all. You look wonderful."

"Good. I'll just pay for this lot and we can go and have some lunch," she said, realising suddenly how hungry she was.

They went to a nice little restaurant at the back of Harrods where Katrina had been before with Charles. It was run by a French couple and the food was simple but delicious. As they drank their coffee after the meal Penny said,

"How's Sarah by the way? Is she back at work?"

"Yes, she's much better. She's not being sick any more, which was the main problem obviously. I had a word with Mark and told him not to let her do too much. I don't think he was quite ready for her being sick. Neither of them have had anything to do with babies, though of course Mark saw you when you had your two, but then you were so well."

124

Suddenly out of the corner of her eye Katrina noticed Sonja heading straight for them. She prayed that she hadn't noticed them. She did not feel like a confrontation

"Keep your head down, Penny," she hissed. "Charles' Sonja is headed straight for us and I really don't want to see her at the moment."

Penny did as she was told but it was too late, Sonja had spotted them. "Hello Katrina," she said loudly. "Fancy seeing you here."

Katrina looked up in mock surprise. "Hello, Sonja, I don't believe you know my daughter, Penny."

"How do you do, Penny," she replied quickly, giving Penny a cursory glance. Turning back to Katrina she continued, "In town for some shopping?"

"Yes, there's always a better choice up here I always find."

"Quite. How's Charles?"

Katrina suddenly realised that Charles had not told Sonja about the wedding. Thank goodness she hadn't mentioned it. What was Charles playing at? Why hadn't he told her?

"Charles is fine, thank you," she replied as casually as she could. "We are meeting him for drinks later and all travelling home together."

"How cosy," Sonja retorted. "Well, I must be off. Things to do, people to see. Bye." She was gone. Katrina sighed with relief.

"So that's the famous Sonja," said Penny watching the retreating figure. "Doesn't she know about the wedding?"

"Apparently not. I don't know why Charles hasn't told her. He promised he would."

"Maybe he thinks she will take it badly and is putting it off. I presume she's not coming to the ceremony."

"I jolly well hope not!" Katrina retorted. "I'm sure she'd make trouble if she did. She went out to America to see him when he was over there, you know. She'd love to break us up if she could."

"But they've been divorced for ages."

"I know but she still seems to think he might go back to her."

125

"What a woman," exclaimed Penny. "Good dresser though."

They laughed and decided to talk about something else. Penny could see that her mother was upset by the encounter.

Later that evening, when Charles and Katrina were alone sipping their nightcaps, she decided that she had better tackle the subject of Sonja and get it over with.

"Guess who we met in London," she began.

"It's too late for guessing games," protested Charles. "Who?"

"Sonja," she replied. "Apparently you haven't told her about the wedding."

Charles looked awkward. "No," he admitted. "I've been busy."

"That's not much of an excuse," Katrina retorted. "Luckily I didn't say anything to her when we met, but I do think she ought to know."

"Yes, I suppose so," agreed Charles sheepishly. "I'm just trying to find a good moment."

"Fine," said Katrina feeling cross that he didn't seem to be making much effort. "She's going to find out in the end and it will be much worse if somebody else tells her," she insisted.

"I suppose you're right. I wish she wasn't such a problem."

They sat in silence for a long time, both deep in thought. Katrina felt utterly miserable. When would this wretched woman stop popping up in their lives to upset them? It wasn't fair.

Katrina went to work next day still feeling upset, having slept badly. Charles hadn't stayed the night, making some excuse about having to get up very early because of a meeting in town. Sue noticed her friend's bad mood and tried to jolly her out of it.

"This will never do," she said. "Two weeks to the wedding of the year and the bride is looking as if she has the troubles of the world on her shoulders. Didn't you have a good day with Penny?"

"Oh, yes, we had a very good day, until we bumped into Sonja. Charles hadn't told her about the wedding, and when we got home I got cross with him about it. He is just scared of telling her. It's ridiculous."

"Why does she have to know?"

"Because if she finds out from someone else she will be furious, and when she gets furious there is no telling what she might do."

"She can't be that bad."

"She's a spiteful witch, who thinks Charles is still her property. The awful thing is that Charles still seems to feel responsible for her. It's crazy. Is she going to haunt us for the rest of our lives?"

"It all seems a bit dramatic to me, but then I have never met the woman. I'm sure you will feel much better when you and Charles are married. He will be really yours then, and you will feel more secure."

"I hope you're right. Apart from calling off the wedding there is nothing much I can do about it anyway."

"You can't do that," exclaimed Sue in horror. "I've just spent a fortune on a new outfit!"

They laughed together and Katrina began to feel better.

"What would I do without you Sue? Thanks for being such a good friend. Well, what's this outfit like then?"

"Wait and see," she replied mysteriously.

"OK be like that," laughed Katrina. "Now what's to be done in this great emporium today?"

"I've got to go to the bank this morning so if you could just hold the fort for a while."

Sue went off and Katrina settled behind the big desk to make a list of things that had to be done over the next fortnight. There wasn't a lot, really, but she kept worrying that she was going to forget something. The little bell rang over the door and Katrina, looking up, was amazed to see Peter standing there. To her great surprise she felt nothing. No embarrassment, no anger, nothing. It was very strange. Sarah had been right, now she had Charles, Peter didn't bother her any more

"Hello Peter. What a surprise to see you here. Is this a social visit, or should I jump up and try and sell you something?"

127

"Hello Katrina. No, don't bother to get up. It's just a social call. Penny told me you were working here so I thought I would just pop in and wish you well for your forthcoming marriage."

Katrina was quite amazed. She wondered if he had some ulterior motive.

"Thank you, Peter, how kind of you," she replied as graciously as she could.

"There was just one more thing I wanted to say to you," he continued, looking rather embarrassed now. Here it comes, thought Katrina, the ulterior motive.

"In the next few days you will be getting a letter from my solicitor to say that your maintenance will be terminated as soon as you marry. I wanted to tell you myself before you got the letter. It's nothing personal, it's just the way things are done."

Peter obviously expected her to get very upset about this piece of news and she let him stand there for a while, worrying, then she said, "Thank you, Peter. I do appreciate the fact that you came to see me, but I did realise that this would happen. Don't worry, I'm not going to get cross and throw things at you. In fact, I would like to thank you for being so generous for all this time."

He relaxed and even managed a smile. "That's all right then. Well, I must be off and leave you to get on. I hope the sun shines for your wedding."

"Thanks, Peter. Bye."

When he had gone Katrina sat back in her chair and marvelled at how her feelings for Peter had changed. Three years ago she had been hiding in doorways rather than meet him. Now she could talk to him without any problems. She was glad he had come to see her to wish her well, and that she had been able to thank him for all her maintenance payments. He could easily have stopped them when she got Emily's money, but he carried on. Hopefully they could be friends now and forget all the trauma they had gone through.

CHAPTER EIGHT

On the following evening, which was a Saturday, Charles and Katrina sat on the settee in front of a roaring fire, feeling rather bloated and lethargic after their meal. An old Frank Sinatra record was playing in the background and they felt very cosy as the wind and rain lashed against the windows outside.

"Do you realise that this time in two weeks we shall be married?" asked Katrina dreamily snuggling into Charles's shoulder.

"The thought had crossed my mind," he replied nonchalantly. "Do you think we have made all the arrangements necessary for the big day?"

"I think so. I hope so. I thought I would just go and see Mr Pan next week and tell him I might be moving again. He's such an old sweetie and he doesn't seem to have any other visitors."

"You're very kind to him. I hope he appreciates it."

"I think he does, his old face certainly light up when I go in."

"I'm not surprised, being visited by such a charming, kind, good looking woman" he retorted.

"Oh sir, you're too kind," she replied primly, grinning happily at his compliment.

"Talking of telling people about the wedding, you will be glad to hear I am going to see Sonja on Monday, after work, and taking her out for a slap up meal. I can't say I am looking forward to it. She's bound to make an awful fuss when she hears we are getting married. Where she gets the idea that she and I will ever get together again, I shall never know."

"Poor Charles. Never mind, maybe she'll surprise you and take the news without her usual histrionics."

"Small chance, I'm afraid."

They sat in silence for a while, deep in their own thoughts. Katrina began to wonder whether perhaps she should have just let things take their course and not insisted that Sonja should be told. Well, it was too late now. Suddenly the phone rang and jolted them both out of their reverie. Katrina went to answer it wondering who on earth it could be at that time of night.

"Hello, Katrina Blackwell speaking."

"Mum, this is Mark. Sorry to bother you so late. It's Sarah, she's back in hospital," there was a catch in his voice as he continued. "She's lost the baby."

Katrina's heart sank. After all the sickness and depression Sarah had gone through and all for nothing. "Oh Mark, I am so sorry. You must be devastated. Do you want me to come up and see her?"

"Could you? She's been asking for you. They gave her a sedative and she's asleep now, but if you could come up tomorrow. I'm sure you must be very busy with all your wedding arrangements but I would be grateful if you could find the time."

"Of course, darling. I'll come tomorrow morning. Are you staying overnight?"

"No, they've told me to go home. There's nothing I can do here if she's asleep. She has to see the doctor in the morning, then I shall probably take her home."

"OK. I'll see you in the hospital first thing tomorrow then. Try and get some sleep. Night darling." She rang off wishing there was something she could do but realising that she would have to wait till morning. She returned to the sitting room.

"What on earth is the matter?" asked Charles seeing her stricken expression.

"Sarah has lost her baby," answered Katrina sitting down again and burying her head in her hands.

"Oh no! After all her troubles, I thought everything was all right again."

"So did we all but apparently not. It's not fair is it?"

"Will you be going up to London to see them?"

"Yes, tomorrow morning. Sarah has had a sleeping pill so there is no point in my going tonight."

"No quite. I wish I could drive you up. It's at times like this that I really curse this useless arm of mine." Charles spat out the words feeling utterly frustrated that he couldn't be more helpful.

"Never mind," said Katrina sympathising with his frustration. "It shouldn't be a bad drive on a Sunday morning with hardly any traffic. I wonder if Sarah will want to come and stay again."

"Will you be able to manage with the wedding so close?"

"I expect so, though I don't think I can take any more time off work. I could always come home at lunchtime and see Sarah is OK. Anyway, perhaps she won't want to come. We shall cross that bridge when we get to it."

"How about a nightcap now," suggested Charles. "You look as if you could do with one."

"What a fine idea," agreed Katrina settling back into the settee. "Sorry the evening has been spoiled, Charles. Never mind. In two weeks we shall be in the Seychelles soaking up the sun."

"Just as well all this happened before we went away. It would be awful to have to fly home as soon as we arrived."

"True. I do wish Sarah's mother was being more supportive. I am quite happy to go up and try and reassure the poor girl, but I don't feel it's really my place somehow."

"I see what you mean. May be they will all patch up their differences now there is no baby involved. We can but hope."

Next morning Katrina set off for London. As she had anticipated the roads were clear, so she made good time. Charles had offered to come with her but she dissuaded him, telling him he would only get bored sitting about the hospital. Deep down he was very grateful that he didn't have to go. He had seen enough of hospitals to last him a lifetime. Katrina had phoned Penny to tell her the news before she left. She had also offered to accompany her mother, but again Katrina had declined the offer. She wanted to talk to Sarah alone if she could. Mark had said she particularly wanted to see her, and she was the only one who knew that Sarah had not wanted the baby.

Katrina found the ward where Sarah had spent the night without too much trouble. She went in and found Mark sitting beside the bed talking earnestly to a very tearful Sarah. They both looked up as she approached and did their best to give her a welcoming smile.

131

Mark got up, gave his mother a kiss and said, "Morning, Mum. Thanks for coming. We are just waiting for the doctor."

Katrina went across and gave Sarah a kiss and a hug. She looked very pale and her eyes were red with crying.

"I'm so sorry about the baby. How are you feeling?" she asked.

"A lot better than I did last night, thank goodness. I'll be better still when they let me go home."

Katrina turned to her son, not wanting him to feel left out. "Did you get a good sleep?" she asked.

"Not too bad, thank you," he replied.

Katrina drew up a chair and sat by the bed.

"Do you want to go and get some breakfast?" she asked Mark. "I can hold the fort here if you like."

"Thanks, Mum. I could do with some coffee, I must say. Will you be all right, Sarah, if I go off?" he asked, holding her hand and looking intently into her sad face.

"Yes, of course. You go and have a good breakfast. The doctor will probably be ages yet. I shall be fine."

Mark got up gratefully and wandered off to find refreshment. When he was out of sight, Katrina turned to Sarah and said, "Now, tell me, what exactly happened? Mark didn't go into any details on the phone."

"Well, the day started like any other Saturday. We had a bit of a lie in, then after breakfast we set off to do the shopping. Half way round the supermarket I started getting these pains. At first I thought it was just indigestion, but it got worse, then I realised I was bleeding. We just dumped our half filled trolley and Mark drove me to the hospital as quickly as he could. It was awful. I was so scared. The staff at the hospital were wonderful, but it seems there was nothing they could do to stop the miscarriage. Oh Katrina, I feel so guilty."

Sarah lay back on her pillows sobbing into her handkerchief. Katrina got up from her chair and put her arm round the poor distressed young woman. Sarah clung to her, sobbing onto her shoulder. When she became a little calmer Katrina asked, "Why are you guilty? It's not your fault. It's just one of those things that happen in this unfair world."

Sarah lay back on her pillows and took a deep breath. "Don't you see," she said staring at Katrina with red-rimmed eyes. "I didn't really want to have this baby. I didn't think I could cope, and my parents are hardly speaking to me because of the pregnancy. Now I've lost the baby I want it more than I could have imagined. I can't speak to Mark properly, because I don't want him to ever know how I felt. He's been so supportive and loving it makes me feel more guilty than ever."

Katrina sat back in her chair and tried to digest all that Sarah had said. She had thought that after Sarah's time with Timothy she had felt more confident about having her own baby but apparently she had still had deep fears. The saddest thing was that she couldn't speak to Mark about it. She must have been under a terrible strain dealing with it all by herself. Her parents hadn't helped either, by the sound of things. She tried to think of something comforting to say.

"Sarah, you have gone through a terrible experience. Any mother who loses a baby feels guilty that she has done something wrong to cause the miscarriage, but truly you can't blame yourself for just thinking you weren't ready for motherhood. I think the most important thing now is for you to tell Mark everything, otherwise your relationship will suffer. There will always be a kind of wall between you. I presume that you still want to go on living with him?"

"Oh yes."

"Well then, when you get home talk the whole thing through with him. Tell him how scared you were about having the baby. You are very young. Perhaps you should leave the idea of having a child for the moment." Katrina was tempted to say that getting married first might help but thought better of it. It sounded too much like Sarah's mother.

There was a long silence while Sarah thought through what Katrina had advised. She still didn't feel she was brave enough to talk to Mark about her fears but, on the other hand, she could see what Katrina had meant by a wall. Finally she said, "You're right, of

133

course, and I will try. Thanks Katrina, I always feel so much better when I have spoken to you. Now I think I shall go to the bathroom and try and patch my face up a bit before Mark comes back."

"Are you allowed out of bed?" asked Katrina anxiously.

"Oh yes, they don't allow you to sit around these days," laughed Sarah putting on her dressing gown and getting out of bed. Before going off to the bathroom she gave Katrina a little kiss on her cheek and said, "Thanks for listening to all my woes. Have you ever thought of taking up counselling?"

They laughed. Mark came back just in time to see Sarah disappearing down the corridor. He sat back on his chair and turned to his Mother.

"Well, I must say I feel better for that coffee. Did you have a good heart to heart talk with Sarah?" he asked.

"Yes, thanks, darling. Poor girl is feeling pretty awful but I think having another woman to talk to helped a bit. It's so terrible that her mother isn't being a bit more supportive. I feel she is the one who should be here talking to Sarah, not me."

"Well, I'm sure you did a grand job anyway," he insisted. "Now where on earth is that doctor? It would be nice to get Sarah home."

"Is she going to be all right tomorrow by herself when you are at work do you think? She could come and stay with me again if you like."

"No, don't worry. I'm sure you have a thousand things to do for this wedding of yours. I'll take the day off tomorrow anyway. Can you stay for lunch – if we are away from here by then, that is?"

"Yes, thank you, that would be nice. What are you going to do about your shopping?"

"I can do that tomorrow, we have some food in the house."

"Fine. I'll go home after lunch then."

Sarah came back from the bathroom looking more like her old self, smiling and beautifully made up. Mark grinned broadly when he caught sight of her and said, "Come here, you gorgeous thing, and give me a hug."

At that moment the doctor came into the ward and was amused to find his patient wrapped tightly round her partner kissing him passionately. He cleared his throat loudly to get her attention and remarked, "Well, this is a big improvement on last night I must say! I gather you are feeling better, Sarah."

Sarah reluctantly broke away from Mark's embrace and replied,
"Yes, thank you, much better. Can I go home now?"

"First I should just like to examine you quickly, to make sure you are fit to go. Perhaps your visitors could wait outside for a moment." He began to draw the curtains round the bed and the nurse came over from the desk to chaperone. Mark and Katrina went outside to wait. In a short while the doctor came out to tell them that Sarah could go home. He told Mark that Sarah would probably get depressed from time to time about the miscarriage, but this was perfectly normal. Mark thanked him for all his trouble and went back into the ward to collect Sarah.

Mark drove Sarah home and Katrina followed in her own car. When they arrived Sarah was made comfortable on the settee, while Mark and Katrina went into the kitchen to try and find something for lunch. As they prepared the meal Mark asked, "How are all the wedding plans going Mum? It's not long now."

"Fine, I think. I just hope we haven't forgotten something. It all seems to have been so easy somehow."

"You and Charles are just very efficient, I expect."

"Did you ask the doctor about Sarah coming to the wedding by the way?"

"Yes. He said see how she feels basically. Don't let her overdo it. I'm sure she'll be OK. She's so looking forward to it."

"I must say, I would hate her to miss it too. It will be so wonderful to have all my family together on my big day, and I do count her as family now. Is that a bit premature?"

Mark laughed and replied, "Whether we get married or not, I can't see Sarah and I splitting up if that's what you want to know."

"Good, that's what I wanted to know."

After a good meal of pork chops and ice cream to follow they all sat in the sitting room with their coffee. Sarah had insisted that she was not hungry, but had still managed to eat a good meal when it was placed before her. Katrina was very pleased to see how much better she was looking.

"Now, you two, are you going to be all right if I go home soon and leave you to it? I'd rather not drive in the dark if I can help it," Katrina asked as she finished her drink.

"Of course, Mum, we'll be fine, won't we, Sarah?" replied Mark.

Sarah nodded. "Thanks so much for coming over and helping with the lunch," she added.

"Do phone if you want a chat any time, won't you?" offered Katrina, hoping that Sarah would ring and tell her that she had had a long talk with Mark about how she had felt, and cleared the air.

"Thanks. It's nice to know that you're there," Sarah replied with a smile.

Katrina got her coat and kissed the young people goodbye adding, "Good luck, Sarah. Just take it easy. I hope to see you both at the wedding."

She drove home secretly pleased that Sarah had refused her invitation to stay. It was not that she was any trouble, it was just that having someone staying in the house meant regular meals and less freedom to do what she wanted when she wanted.

On Monday morning she went into work, feeling tired after her trip to London. She told Sue all about Sarah losing the baby and she was very sad to hear the news.

"Seems to me that that baby was not meant to be," she remarked. "Sarah seems to have had problems from the beginning, what with all the sickness and the trouble with her parents. Let's hope the two of them have a good heart to heart and sort things out between them. They are such a lovely couple."

"My sentiments entirely," agreed Katrina. "I do hope Sarah will be feeling up to coming to the wedding. By the way have Darren and Tracy sorted out their clothes for the big day?"

"Oh yes. They went off together on Saturday and bought their outfits round to show me in the evening. All very smart, surprisingly."

"Good, I'm so pleased they're coming."

"Is Charles having a stag night?"

"No. I think his friends at work would have liked one, but he wasn't keen. He says he's too old for all that nonsense."

"I can see his point," Sue agreed. "You don't want him suffering from a hangover on Saturday anyway, do you?"

"True," laughed Katrina picturing in her mind Charles, staggering into the registry office holding his head and looking ill.

"Now, to get back to business," Sue continued. "I have an idea at the back of my mind, and now that you own a part share in the shop, I thought I should talk it over with you, if I can get your mind off the wedding that is."

Katrina sat up very straight on her chair and put on a serious face. "I'm all ears," she announced.

Sue laughed and went on, "How do you feel about us branching out and taking on a new shop?" she enquired.

Katrina was quite taken aback. She thought about Sue's proposal for a minute or two and then replied, "Are we doing that well? We don't want to overstretch ourselves and end up in trouble."

"Don't worry. We're doing fine, and I'm not going to rush into anything. You know enough about the business now to manage one shop and I'll do the other. I thought that we could get someone to work part time and help out where needed. It would mean that you would be working full time though. What do you think?"

Sue sat back in her chair and watched her friends face, trying to gauge her reaction. Finally Katrina said, "You have obviously been thinking about this for a while. On the whole I think it's a great idea but..."

"Oh dear, I thought I had covered everything," exclaimed Sue.

"But," Katrina continued, "I shall soon be married and wanting to see as much of Charles as possible. You see my problem?"

"Ah," said Sue, pensively. "I'll tell you what, we could close one shop on Saturdays and just keep the other one open. How about that?"

"But Saturday is our busiest time."

"True, but I can't see any other way round can you?"

137

"No, not really. Can I have a bit of time to talk it over with Charles?"

"Yes, of course. Perhaps the answer is to advertise for someone quite new, if you just want to keep going on a part time basis. I just thought you might like to get more involved and have more responsibility," said Sue, rather tersely.

Katrina felt she had unwittingly upset her friend but she really didn't want to work full time and take on a whole new shop just as she was starting a new life with Charles. She was probably being old fashioned and unadventurous, but too bad. It was her life. Anyway, she would see what Charles thought.

"Don't look so worried Katrina, we'll work something out," insisted Sue, not wanting to have a fight with her friend. "Someone named Sophie is coming to help out while you are away, if she's any good perhaps I'll ask her. She's very young but she has worked in the retail clothes business since she left school. Do you want to give up work altogether?" she asked, hoping that all her future plans would not have to be shelved, but suddenly understanding Katrina's new status would change things.

"Oh no," replied Katrina decisively. "I just don't want to take on anything extra just at the moment."

Sue breathed a sigh of relief. "Great. I thought I was going to lose you altogether for a moment there."

"No chance," beamed Katrina. "You're stuck with me, mate." They laughed and went onto the shop to start the day's work.

That evening, as they were locking up Katrina suddenly remembered that Charles was taking Sonja out to supper. She hoped breaking the news of the wedding wasn't going to be too hard for him. Sue told her firmly not to get so worried.

"What do you expect her to do to him?" she asked, "beat him up?"

"Oh no. Sonja is much more subtle than that."

Katrina had to wait till the following evening to hear all the details of the encounter. She was just getting the meal ready for the two of them when Charles wandered in through the back door, looking fatigued after his day in London. After he had given her a big kiss she asked, "Well how did it go with Sonja?"

138

"OK. She was very calm actually. Mind you, I did wait till she had had a good meal and quite a quantity of wine before telling her."

"Wise move. I'm glad it wasn't too bad. Now how about some supper? I'll just strain this spaghetti and we'll be ready."

"Great, I feel in need of nourishment," replied Charles taking off his jacket. "Can I get you a drink?"

"Yes, please. There's wine on the table."

Later, as they were drinking their coffee Katrina said,"I have some news for you. Sue has decided to open another shop. She asked me yesterday if I would be prepared to work full time and run one shop if she ran the other. It was quite a surprise."

"Are you sure you want to take on the extra work? I was hoping that you might work less when we were married."

"I thought you would say that so I turned down the idea. I'm afraid she was a bit upset. She has obviously been hatching this plan for a while and thought I would be thrilled."

"Oh dear. Well, I'm glad we both feel the same anyway. Has Sue got a new property in mind?"

"I don't think so. As a part owner of the company she felt I should be told her plans before she went any further, I think."

"Well, I'm glad she's doing so well that she is thinking of expanding. I just hope she's not overstretching herself."

"I don't think so. She's pretty good at making money. As long as she doesn't meet another Patrick," said Katrina, remembering the reason for her financial involvement with Sue's shop.

"Quite," agreed Charles laughing. "Now, enough of high finance, have you heard from Sarah?"

"No. I just hope that no news is good news. I've been in all day, so I can't have missed her."

"I hope you're right. By the way, before I forget, could you phone the hotel tomorrow and ask for one vegetarian meal at the reception? Apparently Jim's wife doesn't eat meat."

"Of course. Could you go through your friend's names again? I keep forgetting."

139

"Jim is married to Gloria, and Pete is married to Chris, OK?"

They sat on, chatting about the wedding, checking on the details for the big day until it was time for bed. Later, as Katrina lay back, after some intense and energetic love-making, she decided that she was immensely happy with her lot. Beside her Charles was snoring gently, and she snuggled closer to him, fitting into the curled shape of his sleeping body. Everything seemed to be going so well, apart from a slight worry about Mark and Sarah at the back of her mind. She could hardly wait for the wedding and the honeymoon, and then the prospect of setting up a new shop. It was all too good to be true.

Next day she drove out to the nursing home to see Mr Pan. It was a fine bright day, for a change, and she drove with the window down, breathing in the fresh smell of the countryside after all the rain they had had lately. She prayed that she would have such a day for her wedding. She found Mr Pan sitting in the lounge beside a rather wizened old lady, deep in conversation.

"Hello Mr Pan," she said bending down slightly, so that he could see her. He immediately looked up and gave her his usual enormous grin.

"Hello, Katrina. How kind of you to come." Pointing to his companion he continued, "I don't believe you know my friend, Zilla."

"Hello, Zilla, Nice to meet you," Katrina replied, studying the strange looking little lady. She looked as if she would be more at home in a gypsy caravan than sitting there in the lounge of the old people's home. She was dressed in black from head to toe, and wore a scarf on her head, tied in a gypsy fashion. Her fingers were covered in rings and round her neck she wore gold necklaces. Her face was nut brown, wrinkled and weathered by years of outdoor living. 'I wish I could paint,' thought Katrina, what a wonderful face and those piercing blue eyes that seemed to look straight into your soul.

"How do you do, Katrina," she said. "Mr Pan has told me all about you."

"All good, I hope," laughed Katrina awkwardly, feeling embarrassed by those piercing eyes staring at her.

"Of course," replied Mr Pan enthusiastically. "Zilla used to be with a circus, you know. She can read palms, tell your fortune and that sort of thing. Would you like your palms read?"

Katrina hesitated. She had always been rather wary of fortune tellers. She felt that she would rather not know what was in store, however she didn't want to upset the old people.

"OK," she said offering her upturned hands to Zilla, feeling her heart beating faster.

Zilla studied her palms carefully, running her long thin fingers over the lines. At last she said, "You have a long lifeline, Katrina, but you have many troubles on the way. Your son has just had a big sorrow which has made you sad too."

Katrina was amazed. How on earth could Zilla know about Sarah losing the baby?

"A lady with a red dress is going to bring you great trouble. You will have to be very strong," the old lady continued. "That's all I can do for now," she said dropping Katrina's hand, and looking into her eyes for a moment. A shiver went down Katrina's back. She wished she had refused to have the reading, after all it hadn't told her much except to beware of a lady in a red dress.

"Thank you, Zilla. Have you been here long?" Katrina asked trying to get back to a normal conversation.

"Not long, but too long. I like to be in the open, but my legs are so bad that I have to stay here now," replied the old lady, with sadness in her voice. Katrina felt very sorry for her. She was like a bird in a cage.

"At least you have Mr Pan to cheer you up. He felt like you when he first came but he's a lot happier now, aren't you?" she said turning to the old man.

Mr Pan grinned. "I'll look after you Zilla," he said taking her hand. Katrina noticed Zilla relax a bit and give him a little smile.

"Perhaps we could take Zilla to see your lovely garden sometime," Katrina suggested.

Mr Pan agreed he would like that. The tea came then and Katrina prayed that Zilla would not want to read her tea leaves. She'd had enough of predictions for one day. She needn't have worried. She told Mr Pan about her plans for moving from "his"

141

house. His main concern seemed to be that she would go on visiting him from time to time. She assured him she would still come. She and Charles were not planning to move far. She told him about his garden and the fact that the daffodils were already showing through, and the winter jasmine was still in flower. He seemed less interested than he had been when Katrina first visited him. He had other interests now to take the place of his old garden.

After a while the conversation began to dry up and Katrina decided it was time she was going. She shook hands with Mr Pan and Zilla, and promised to go and see them again when she got back from her honeymoon. She walked across the car park towards her car taking deep breaths of air, pleased to be on her way. It had been a rather spooky afternoon.

That evening Sarah phoned. Mark was in the bath so she could talk freely.

"I took your advice," she began, "and had a long talk with Mark about how I had felt when I was pregnant. He was very understanding and I wished I had spoken earlier, rather than bottle it all up. I am still feeling a bit wobbly and find myself bursting into tears over silly things, but on the whole I'm not feeling too bad."

"That is good news, Sarah. How are things with your parents?"

"They're still a bit cool, but we are going over for lunch on Sunday, so hopefully things are getting back to normal. Mark and I have decided that perhaps we should get married, follow your example."

"That's wonderful news, Sarah. Congratulations," said Katrina, thrilled that the miscarriage had not had a detrimental effect on the relationship. In fact it seemed to have cemented it if anything.

"Well, I'd better ring off now and go and finish making the supper," announced Sarah. "We shall look forward to seeing you at the wedding. Bye."

"Thanks for ringing, Sarah. See you at the wedding." Katrina put down the receiver and sat for a long time thinking over Sarah's news. She hoped she and Mark were not rushing into marriage to please her parents. Well, time would tell.

142

The following Sunday Katrina went to Penny's for lunch. Charles had also been asked, but had declined the invitation on the grounds that he had some extra paperwork to do before his holiday. Katrina drove herself to the house through the empty streets, looking forward to a family day, and wondering how Mark and Sarah were getting on. She hoped that now Sarah was no longer pregnant, and the two of them were thinking of getting married, that things would go better with Sarah's parents.

She parked her car and walked up the drive to Penny's house. Before she had time to ring the bell Josh had the door open and was giving his grandmother a big hug.

"Hello, Josh," said Katrina, trying not to drop the cake she was holding. "Let me take this cake into the kitchen and then I can give you a proper hug."

They went into the kitchen, where Max was helping his mother count the potatoes for lunch. Katrina put her cake down and gave everyone a hug.

"We're coming to your wedding next week," announced Max. "Would you like to come and see our new suits?"

Penny and Katrina laughed.

"Yes, come on, Grandma," insisted Josh as the two boys took her hands and led her upstairs to see their new clothes. Katrina admired the little navy suits and told them how proud she would be to see them so smartly dressed at her wedding.

"Why are you getting married?" asked Josh. "Aren't you too old?"

Katrina laughed at the directness of her young grandson, then she put on a very serious face and said, "No one is too old to get married Josh. I agree most people get married when they are young but not everyone. Charles and I love each other very much and want to live together for ever and ever, so we are getting married."

Josh thought about this for a moment and then said, "I see. Will Charles be my new grandpa?"

"Yes, I suppose he will. Though I think he would still like to be called Charles."

"We will have three grandmas and three grandpas," said Max, not wanting to be left out of the conversation.

"That's right," agreed Katrina, "Aren't you lucky boys? Now let's go down and help your Mummy with the lunch shall we?"

Later that day Katrina told Penny about her conversation with the boys and added, "It must be quite confusing for them to understand why they have three sets of grandparents, but they seem to have come to terms with it. I'm glad that Charles is so fond of them. He is really thrilled to be getting a new family."

"You have made a good choice there, Mum. I'm so pleased for you. You deserve a bit of fun and security and I'm sure Charles will look after you well. He's such a charming man."

"I must agree with you there. I am getting quite excited about becoming Mrs Harris."

"Let's hope the weather clears a bit for next Saturday," said Penny looking out at the pouring rain." It makes such a difference to these occasions when the sun shines."

"True, but I don't think I shall really care when the time comes. After all, we have got two weeks in the Seychelles to look forward to."

"Lucky things. Wish we could come too."
Katrina laughed, "Much as I love you all, this holiday is for me and Charles only. You'll just have to stay jealous."

"Meanie! Two weeks in the sun would have really been nice in the middle of this horrid winter. By the way, have you heard from Mark and Sarah? Will she be well enough for the wedding?"

"I think so. The doctor seems happy for her to come if she feels up to it. We shall just have to keep an eye on her to see that she doesn't overdo it. Don't say anything, because it's a bit of a secret as yet, but I gather that they are talking about getting married. Isn't that great?"

"Mum, that's wonderful! I promise I won't say a word. When did you hear?"

"Only last week. They are having lunch with Sarah's parents today so if they tell them, perhaps they will make it official after that."

"Yippee, another wedding," said Penny dancing round the room.

144

CHAPTER NINE

The next few days flew by for Katrina. She went into work on Monday as usual and was amazed that news of her forthcoming wedding had spread amongst the regular customers. Several of them came in with cards and one or two even bought her small gifts. She was thrilled that so many people should care about her welfare.

After work she and Sue decided to go to the Bistro for supper. The waiter, who showed them to a free table, greeted them like old friends.

"Haven't seen you two for ages. I hope that you were busy and not taking your business elsewhere."

"How could you think such a thing," exclaimed Sue with a wide grin. "We wouldn't dream of going any where else." They ordered wine and took the menus from the waiter.

"It is ages since we went out for a meal together. Do you think Charles will give you a night off from time to time, once you're married?"

"I think we shall have to have business conferences, don't you?" suggested Katrina grinning broadly.

"What a good idea!" agreed Sue. "After all, we shall have a lot to discuss as our Empire grows."

They both giggled and, as the wine arrived, drank a toast to their expanding business.

"Talking of the new shop, have you seen any likely properties yet?" enquired Katrina.

"No, but I have put my name down with various agents. It could take a while."

"No point in rushing, is there? May as well take your time and get exactly what you want."

"Exactly, though if something comes up while you're away do you mind if I go ahead?"

"Of course not. You have much more experience at this sort of thing than me. No, you go ahead if you find anything."

"Fine. I just didn't want to go over your head if you weren't happy. Now, on to more immediate things, how are you feeling about Saturday?"

"I must admit to a sense of panic from time to time. Silly really. I know I love Charles but do I want to marry him? Most days I do but then I suddenly wonder if I shall miss my independence."

"You're bound to have to make adjustments," agreed Sue thoughtfully. "I don't think I should want to marry again, but then I'm not you. You are much more of a homebody than I shall ever be. You just have to weigh up the pros and cons and follow your instincts. After all you spend most of your free time together anyway. Being married isn't going to be that different."

They sat in silence for a while, eating their meal. Sue was rather surprised that Katrina was getting cold feet. She and Charles had always seemed such a perfect pair, in spite of their ups and downs.

When the meal was finished Sue produced a large box from under the table and handed it to Katrina.

"Oh Sue, thank you," she said gazing at the beautifully wrapped parcel. "I hardly like to undo it; it's such a work of art."

"Don't be silly. Come on undo it and tell me if you like it," insisted Sue impatiently.

Katrina did as she was told and found, nestling amongst the layers of tissue paper, a superb white silk nightdress embroidered with tiny pink rosebuds round the yoke. She took it out of the box and held the wonderful material against her cheek.

"What a fantastic present," she enthused, grabbing her friend and hugging her tightly. "Thank you, thank you, it's perfect."

"I'm so glad you like it," said Sue beaming from ear to ear. "I'm sure you and Charles have everything you need for the house so I thought I would get you something personal. Knowing you two, I don't expect you will wear it much on the honeymoon but it could come in handy later," said Sue with a big grin.

"I hope you are not implying that Charles and I are sex mad!" replied Katrina pompously, returning the magnificent garment to its box.

"Of course not! Just human and in love," retorted Sue.

146

Katrina sat back in her chair and sighed contentedly. She felt quite overwhelmed by all the kindness she had received during the day but it was beginning to take its toll and she suddenly felt very tired.

"I think it's time I was going home," she announced. "It's been a wonderful day but I am beginning to feel in need of my bed."

"I think you have a point there," agreed Sue yawning. "Some of us have to get up early in the morning, too."

"My heart bleeds for you," said Katrina sarcastically. Sue hit her with her table napkin. They got up and left the restaurant, giggling like a couple of schoolgirls.

Next day, Penny arrived with yet another parcel for Katrina and Charles. It was an original watercolour of the park and the lake painted by a local artist. Katrina was thrilled. She loved watercolours and this one would remind her of all the wonderful walks she and Charles and her family had had over the years.

"Thank you so much, Penny," she said kissing her daughter fondly. "It's beautiful."

"I'm so glad you like it, Mum. I saw it recently in an art shop and thought it might be appropriate. Have you and Charles decided where to live yet? Do you want me to hang it for you?"

"No, don't bother now. Charles can do it later. We plan to decide about where to live after the honeymoon. There's no rush."

"Did you go and see Mr Pan, by the way?"

"Yes, I did, and found he has a new girlfriend called Zilla. She is a very strange old lady, wizened like a little prune and brown as a berry. She used to be with a circus, telling fortunes in a little tent, but she has something wrong with her legs and her relations decided they couldn't look after her in a caravan any more. So she has just arrived at the nursing home. She's not happy, but Mr Pan is doing his best to cheer her up. Anyway he insisted that she read my palm. It was very spooky. You know how I hate that sort of thing. I would rather not know what the future holds quite honestly. She seemed to know all about Sarah losing the baby, and told me to beware of a lady in a red dress. Then she gave me a very strange look, as if she knew more than she was telling. She had the most amazing eyes you have ever seen." Katrina felt a chill go down her back at the memory.

"Maybe Mr Pan told her about Sarah's baby," said Penny cynically, trying to explain away Zilla's insight.

"Oh no," replied her mother. "Mr Pan didn't know."

"Well, I expect there is some perfectly sensible explanation. Don't let it worry you, Mum," she continued noticing the look of alarm on her Mothers face. "As for, beware of the lady with the red dress, that could mean anything."

"I'm sorry, you must think I am being very silly, but that little woman really scared me. She looked at me in such a funny way."

"She was a professional fortune teller, she has probably been working on that look for years. Forget it, Mum. Lets talk about something else."

They talked about the boys and how well Josh was doing at school and Katrina began to relax again. By the time Penny left she had forgotten all about Zilla and the red dress.

She hadn't told Charles about what Zilla had said because she thought he would laugh it off, just as Penny had done. Someone who believed in these things had once said that even if you know the future, you can't change it. So what was the point in knowing, Katrina wondered.

The following morning Katrina was sitting trying to get her thank you letters up to date when the phone rang.

"Mrs Blackwell?"

"Yes speaking."

"This is the manager of the County Hotel. Rather bad news, I'm afraid. I notice from my books that you have a wedding reception booked for Saturday, is that right?"

"Yes," agreed Katrina wondering what the problem was.

"Well, I'm afraid we have had a fire in our kitchen and have had to cancel all our bookings for at least the next week."

Katrina's heart sank. Where was she supposed to find a new venue at such short notice?

"We will of course refund your deposit, but with no kitchen we will just not be able to function."

"What do you suggest I do?" asked Katrina beginning to get cross. "The refund is going to do no good at all if there is nowhere for us to go."

"All I can do is offer my sincere apologies, Madam, and wish you luck in your search for a new venue," replied the manager trying to keep cool. He had been making phone calls to irate customers all morning and was beginning to get a headache. Katrina suddenly felt very sorry for him, after all, the situation was not his fault.

"Well, thank you for letting me know," she said wearily. "I suppose I shall just have to phone round and see what I can find." She rang off and sat deep in thought trying to think of what to do next. The wedding was in four days and she was sure that nowhere would have space for fifteen extra guests at this late stage. She phoned Charles and told him the bad news.

"I think I am going to have to do this reception myself after all," she said finally. "I can't think that anywhere half decent will have any spare room for us."

"Have you tried ringing round? I don't want you worn out before the long night flight we've got ahead of us after the wedding."

"All right, I'll try ringing round, but I don't hold out much hope. Thanks for listening. See you tonight."

She went through the yellow pages phoning every restaurant that looked possible but could find no one who would do a wedding reception at such short notice, even a small one for fifteen. In the end she phoned Penny and told her the bad news.

"Will you give me a hand if I do the whole thing at the house?"

"Of course, but is there enough room for everyone?"

Katrina's heart dropped. She had been thinking of food rather than space and she could see now that it would be an awful squash in her little house.

"Oh dear, you're right, of course. What can I do?"

"Don't despair Mum, we'll have your reception here. I will have to just check with James but I'm sure he won't mind. What do you think?"

149

"I think you're an angel," said her Mother with feeling. "Your house would be perfect, but do talk to James before we go any further won't you? And don't pressure him will you?"

"OK Mum, I promise."

Later that day Penny phoned back and said that James had agreed to have the reception in their house.

"What's more," she continued proudly, "I've found you a caterer. She's an old friend of mine who has just started her own business so her bookings are a bit sparse at the moment. She would be thrilled to have the work, if that is OK with you."

"That sounds great, Penny. Gosh, that's a weight off my mind. Can I meet her and discuss food?"

"Yes, of course. I'll bring her over tomorrow morning if that's all right, about ten."

"Fine, look forward to seeing you then. Bye darling and thanks again."

Next morning Penny arrived just after ten with her friend Pamela in tow. As Katrina let them in she had the distinct impression that all was not well. Both women looked very ill at ease for some reason. They took their coats off and sat down in the sitting room, while Katrina went to fetch the coffee. As she handed it round she could feel the tension in the room and wondered what on earth was the matter. Perhaps Pamela was nervous, if she was so new to the business. She suddenly seemed to make a decision and putting her cup down sat up very straight in her chair and looked right at Katrina.

"Mrs Blackmore," she began.

"Katrina, please," interrupted her employer.

"Fine, as you wish," Pamela started again. " Katrina, there is something I have to tell you before we go any further," she continued, looking more nervous than ever. "It's about Charles Harris. Just after he left his wife and came to live down here, he and I were what I believe is now known as an item. We went everywhere together, and even talked about getting married, when the divorce came through. Then Sonja, his estranged wife, heard about our relationship and made our lives hell. She used to phone in the middle of the night to see if Charles was with me, and send me hate mail

150

telling me she would never let Charles marry me. In the end it all got too much for me and we split up. Rather acrimoniously, I'm afraid. I felt he should have stood up to her and told her to behave. Anyway, I haven't seen him since. When Penny told me who you were marrying I thought I should tell you the whole story and save embarrassment. I shall quite understand if you would rather I didn't do the catering."

Katrina sat back in her chair, appalled at what she had heard. Poor Charles. No wonder he hadn't wanted to tell Sonja about the wedding. She suddenly felt very frightened about what Sonja might be planning to do to stop the wedding this time. Then she told herself not to be so silly. Charles had said she had taken the news very calmly. Hopefully she had accepted defeat this time. She looked across to Pamela, who was sitting nervously waiting for her decision on the catering.

"That's quite a story," she began. "Thank you for telling me. I think the best way to handle this is for you to prepare the meal so that we can help ourselves when we get back from the ceremony. That way you and Charles need not meet at all. What do you think?"

Pamela relaxed visibly. She obviously wanted the job but did not want to meet Charles. It was quite understandable in the circumstances.

"Thank you. That would make things easier," she said. "I really don't think I could face meeting him again, especially on his wedding day," taking some papers out of her bag and handing them to Katrina. "Perhaps you would like to choose a menu from one of these. They're all cold buffet meals."

The three of them sat and talked over the arrangements for the next hour. Katrina decided that she liked Pamela very much, and was grateful to her for being so honest. Charles and Pamela bumping into each other at the reception could have spoilt the day completely. She decided not to tell Charles anything about the morning meeting except that they had a very good caterer who was a friend of Penny's. That should suffice.

On the following Friday evening Katrina sat in her sitting room, dressed in her best black frock, waiting for Charles to pick her up and take her out to supper. She felt exhausted after a busy day at

Penny's, cleaning the house and getting things ready for the next day. The last thing she felt like doing was going out to supper with four people she hardly knew. Although Charles had refused to have a stag night he had compromised and agreed to go out for a slap up meal with his close friends from work, and their wives, that evening. Katrina went over their names again in her head. Jim and Gloria, Pete and Chris, not too difficult, but she was so bad with names. They were all going to stay the night with Charles and take him to the registry office the next day.

She went over the arrangements for the wedding in her head. Sue was going to pick her up at the house at ten thirty and drive her to the registry office. The wedding was booked for eleven. She and Charles had a taxi booked to drive them to Penny's house, where the reception would be held. At three o'clock James would drive Charles and herself back to her house to change, then on to the airport. She sighed. In a way she would be glad to be on the plane with this wedding behind her. She remembered her first wedding to Peter, it seemed centuries ago now. She had been so young then and everything had been so exciting. Perhaps tomorrow she would feel differently, but at the moment she just felt flat and tired.

The doorbell rang and she got up to answer it. There stood Charles, looking very handsome in his best suit, and she suddenly realised how much she loved him. Tomorrow would be wonderful. She needn't have worried. Her energy and excitement suddenly returned as he pulled her to him kissed her passionately, and told her how much he loved her and how much he was looking forward to having her as his wife.

"You look wonderful Katrina. Come on, let's get to this party. They are all longing to see you again."

Jim had been to the restaurant before so he had driven the rest of the party on ahead. Katrina and Charles drove through the dark streets in silence, content in each other's company, and both deep in their own thoughts. Katrina was remembering the first time Charles had taken her to the restaurant. She wondered idly if he had ever taken Pamela there.

When at last they arrived, they were greeted on the doorstep by the rest of the party. Charles made the introductions again, just to remind Katrina of the names. They had of course met before at the firm's dinner. Both Jim and Pete were big men, who looked as if they worked out at the gym regularly, in spite of the fact that they both had desk jobs now, like Charles. They greeted her warmly and she felt she had been accepted into "the gang." Gloria was a big friendly woman of about Katrina's age, and was in stark contrast to Chris who was petite and shy and much younger. Perhaps a second wife, thought Katrina. They were shown to their table and Katrina found herself sitting between Jim and Pete. When they had ordered and were sitting back, sipping their aperitifs, Jim turned to Katrina and asked, "Now tell us all about yourself, Katrina. Charles has been very secretive about you up till now and we didn't get much of a chance to talk at the dinner."

"There's nothing much to tell, really," replied Katrina, wondering how much to say without being boring. "I'm a divorced woman with two grown up children and two grandchildren. You'll meet them tomorrow at the wedding, of course. I work part time in a small boutique with my friend Sue, who you will also meet tomorrow. That's about it really."

"How did you first meet Charles?" enquired Gloria. "I always find it so interesting to know how people first meet, don't you?" she continued, addressing the people round the table.

Katrina grinned and decided to make her first meeting with Charles sound very romantic.

"I moved into the house next door to Charles and he bought me round a big bunch of his prize dahlias as a welcome present. I was smitten at once, of course."

They all laughed and Pete remarked,

"Good old Charles. Always did have a good eye for the ladies."

"Now, Pete, I don't want you putting my future bride off with stories of my wicked past," cautioned Charles in mock horror.

"Ah, so you have a wicked past, Charles?" laughed Katrina, winking at him across the table. "Perhaps you should tell me more, Pete."

"Maybe later," replied Pete mysteriously. Just then their meal came and conversation was halted for a while as they ate the delicious food. It was a great evening and Katrina thoroughly enjoyed the company of Charles's friends. She noticed that Chris didn't say a lot but she seemed quite happy to sit back and listen to the general banter. It was past midnight by the time they left the restaurant and although Katrina offered them all nightcaps they declined and instead drove themselves back to Charles's house for a good night rest. Even Charles just kissed her good night on the doorstep, refusing to go in and saying, "See you tomorrow, darling. I hope you enjoyed the evening."

"Yes, thank you. Your friends are great fun aren't they? Is Chris always as quiet as that by the way? She hardly said a word all evening."

"She is a little mouse isn't she? Don't worry. She's always like that. Get her talking about music though and she blossoms. She was a full time professional pianist before she married, but now she just does the odd concert. I'll take you to see her sometime when we're settled."

"I shall look forward to that. Now, you had better go and get some sleep. I'll see you in the registrar's office. Don't be late."

He kissed her again, and returned to his house, hoping that his guests were already in bed. He needed some sleep. Tomorrow was going to be tricky.

Katrina got into bed feeling exhausted but had great difficulty getting off to sleep. Her mind was busy with thoughts of the wedding, the honey moon, the new shop, Mark and Sarah, Sonja... Finally she dozed off, and woke to find the sun streaming through the curtains. She panicked thinking she had overslept, but looking at her bedside clock she found it was only eight o'clock. Plenty of time to be ready for Sue at ten thirty.

She was just finishing her packing when the phone rang.

"Don't panic! It's only me, making sure you are up," said Sue cheerily on the other end. "Did you have a good time last night?"

"Yes, thanks," replied Katrina enthusiastically, thankful that the call was not because of a last minute problem. "Charles's friends are great fun and we had a lovely meal, as usual."

"Good. I shall look forward to meeting them later. No single ones I suppose?" she asked hopefully.

"Dear Sue, always on the look out," teased Katrina. "Sorry, they were all spoken for."

"Never mind, just thought I would ask. See you at ten thirty then. Bye."

The phone rang again almost as soon as she had put it down. This time it was Charles.

"Morning darling. Just phoned to see you were up and to say how much I love you," he explained.

"Love you too," she replied, enthusiastically. "Yes I am up. Don't worry, I won't be late."

"Fine. I'll leave you to it then. Bye."

Next to phone was Penny. She just wanted to say that Pamela had arrived and was setting out the food. It all looked marvellous.

"Thanks for phoning, Penny," said Katrina wondering if she was ever going to get everything done with these constant phone calls. "I'm glad to hear everything is under control. I'd better go now as I still haven't finished my packing."

"OK Mum. See you later."

Katrina returned to her suitcase, hoping that that was the last call. She had thought that she had plenty of time, but suddenly it was going fast. She threw the last few things into her bag and went to have a bath. By ten-thirty, when Sue arrived, she was ready to go.

"Morning, Katrina," said Sue as Katrina let her in. "My, you do look gorgeous. I love that suit. It's just perfect. Now are you ready to go?"

"Yes, I think so. I'm feeling terribly nervous though. Shall we have a sherry before we go?"

"OK, you don't want to look too eager do you?" Katrina poured the drinks and sat down trying to relax. She felt very cross with herself for being so anxious and was very grateful to have Sue there to calm her.

"I don't know why I'm feeling so worried," she remarked to her friend. "After all, everything is going like clockwork. Penny phoned to say that Pamela was setting out the food, and it all looked wonderful. Charles phoned to say he still loved me, and here we are ready to go to the registry office, with a good chance of getting there on time. What could go wrong now?"

"You're nervous because you are getting married again. It's a big step to take, especially as your first marriage ended in divorce. It's only natural."

"I suppose you're right. Thanks for being so down to earth, Sue. By the way you do look lovely this morning. That shade of green really suits you."

"Thanks, Katrina. Now, I think we should be going. Do you feel better for the sherry?"

"Yes, thanks," replied Katrina glancing at her watch. "Goodness it's quarter to, we'll be late."

They rushed from the house and in spite of everything arrived at the registry office just before eleven. The rest of the wedding party had arrived and were standing chatting in the lobby. Charles rushed forward to greet Katrina with a big kiss.

"Darling, you look breathtaking!" he exclaimed, standing back to admire his future wife.

"And you look as handsome as ever," she replied, suddenly feeling calmer.

The other guests all came forward then, to greet her and remark how beautiful she was looking. Josh and Max insisted on having a big kiss then informed her that she would be going to their house after the ceremony to have lunch.

"There's a lady there, getting it all ready," said Josh importantly.

"That will be nice," said Katrina hoping that the boys would not mention the lady's name, but she needn't have worried. She was pleased to see that Mark and Sarah had managed to get to the ceremony and that Sarah was looking much better. She hardly recognised Darren and Tracy, who had really gone to town with their outfits. Darren was in a khaki coloured, baggy suit and Tracy in a long flowing red dress. Surely she wasn't the one Zilla had warned of? Katrina banished the thought almost as soon as she had had it.

Just then the big doors opened, and the previous wedding party spilled out. There were a few moments of confusion, as the two sets of guests tried to get past each other in the small lobby. When the main room was clear again Katrina and Charles led their party in. They sat in front of the big table, with their backs to their guests, and waited for everyone to get seated. The registrar, seated opposite them, quietly explained the procedure, while everyone settled down. At last everything was quiet so Katrina and Charles stood up and the ceremony began. Katrina heard the door open and shut at the back of the hall and wondered who had come in late. She had thought everyone had already arrived when they entered the room. She was looking intently at the registrar and concentrating on her words, when she noticed, out of the corner of her eye, someone running towards Charles, someone in a red dress.

She screamed, as the sound of a gun being fired rang out through the room. Charles fell to the floor and everything seemed to go into slow motion. Pete and Jim ran forward and managed to seize the gun from Sonja's hand and march her from the room. As she was dragged away she turned and screamed at Katrina, "You thought you could take him away from me didn't you! Well, you were wrong!"

The guests rushed forward to see if there was anything they could do as the registrar collapsed into her chair, looking very white and shaken. As the door closed behind Sonja and her escorts Katrina knelt on the floor beside Charles. She could hardly believe her eyes. He was winking at her.

"Come on, Katrina, help me up and let's get on with this wedding," he exclaimed.

Katrina felt the room going round as she lost consciousness.

She came round, at last, to find everyone bending over her. It took a while for her to remember where she was.

"What on earth's going on?" she asked, addressing a very concerned looking Charles. "I thought you were dead."

"So did Sonja. I'm so sorry to have had to put you through all that, but it seemed the only way. I'll tell you the whole story later. Suffice to say I am alive and well and ready to get married. How about you?"

"I feel a bit shaky, but I'll be all right, I think. Help me up will you. Could I have a drink of water please?"

Katrina never could remember the wedding ceremony. The guests had gone back to their places, and the rather shaken registrar had conducted the wedding. She supposed she had made the right responses but in her memory it was all a bit of a blur. Later, as she sat in the taxi with Charles, being driven to Penny's house for the reception, Charles explained what had happened. One of Sonja's close friends had phoned him and said that Sonja had told her that she was planning to shoot Charles at the wedding. She was very scared and didn't know what to do.

Charles knew that Sonja had a gun which she had bought in America, for protection, and that she knew how to use it. She had been to classes and belonged to a club in London, so he took the threat seriously. He and Pete and Jim had made a plan. All of them had worn body armour just in case. They had told the police of their suspicions, but they could do nothing. Sonja had a licence for the gun, so until she actually used it, they were powerless. Charles had pretended to be dead, as otherwise they thought she might start shooting everyone else, if she felt she had failed to kill Charles. Anyway, Sonja was now in custody, arrested for attempted murder, and should give them no more trouble. Katrina sat back in her seat still feeling a little faint. She would be glad when this day was over and she was safely on the plane to the Seychelles. She turned and looked at her new husband.

"I think you must have nine lives, like a cat," she remarked. "You haven't got any more excitements up your sleeve I hope. I don't think I could stand it."

"No," he assured her, kissing her forehead tenderly. "I promise from now on to settle down to quiet domesticity." The taxi came to a stop. "Well, here we are at Penny's. Come on Mrs Harris, let's go and enjoy our party."

They walked up the path together, arm in arm, smiling happily as their waiting guests spilled out of the house to greet them.

BIOGRAPHIES OF MAIN CHARACTERS

KATRINA BLACKWELL

A tall blonde, slim, smart 47 year old. Attractive, but not beautiful. An only child, born to older parents who doted on her. She had a good education and after school went to university where she got a 2-1 in English. Immediately married Peter, much against her parents wishes. They were hoping she would get work and make use of her education. Her first child Penny was born two years after her marriage, and her son Mark two years after that. She was married to Peter for twenty-seven years and was perfectly happy to remain a housewife and mother. She had no ambition to work away from home, which was probably just as well, as Peter thoroughly disapproved of working wives.

As the children got older she started doing charity work, helping to organise fund raising balls, craft fairs and so on. She also went to the gym twice a week to keep herself fit and trim.

She and Peter lived in a well positioned house with five bedrooms, a big garden and a swimming pool. They had never been short of money and enjoyed a good social life. Although Katrina knew a lot of people she had never had a really close friend. She was basically a bit of a loner. When Peter asks for a divorce she is thoroughly shaken and can think of no one to talk to but her daughter. As she suddenly finds herself having to cope with real life for a change, she finds hidden strength and to her amazement, manages to find herself a new way of life.

PETER BLACKWELL

A tall dark man in his early fifties, beginning to get a bit of a paunch, due to frequent business lunches. A man who liked to be in charge, but did not like confrontation, especially at home. Worked in higher management in a computer firm.

Born of rich parents, he had had a good education and also had a university degree. In fact he and Katrina met at university.

Had been faithful to and happy with Katrina until he met Shirley, at a time when he was beginning to feel his age and needed a bit of excitement.

PENNY TAYLOR

Smart twenty-five year old. Eldest child of Katrina and Peter and herself mother of two boys. A kind easy-going person, many close friends, unlike her mother. Very good relationship with both her parents. A tower of strength for her mother when her father left, but still kept in touch with him when he married Shirley.

Very happily married to James, a well-to-do solicitor five years her senior.

Very upset about her parents break up but realised that the only thing she could do was to remain friends with both parents and give support where she could.

MARK BLACKWELL

Twenty-three year old son of Katrina and Peter. Hard working man about town, with a job in the city, and a bachelor flat in London. Much closer to his mother than his father, though he didn't get to see either very often, due to his busy working and social life. Also upset about his parents break up, but not as much as his sister. Has a grand plan not to get married until he is at least thirty. Then he meets and falls in love with Sarah, and his whole life changes.

Kind and helpful to his mother, on his rare visits to see her, but otherwise just keeps in touch by phone. Concerned, but not as involved as his sister.

SARAH SHAW

Early twenties, tall thin willowy blonde. Rather shy. Works in the city with Mark and also lives in London. Falls in love with Mark and moves in with him. Has rather old fashioned parents, who thoroughly disapprove. Has led a very sheltered life but is eager to break away from her parents and make a life for herself. A wizard at numbers, and doing very well in the city.

SUE COOPER

A very tough forty year old single parent, who owns the shop where Katrina eventually gets a job. She walked out on her husband, Sam, when he started to beat her and she has generally had a very hard life due to continuous money problems. She adores her son Darren, in spite of the fact he is always in trouble, and does her best to make a good life for him. When Katrina meets her she has just bought the shop with some money left to her by her grandmother. At first Sue is rather cool with Katrina, but as time goes by they become the best of friends.

In spite of her earlier experiences Sue is always on the look out for a new man who will love her and deal with all her problems, but she is not lucky in love. However, as the business prospers she begins to get more confidence. She has a wonderful eye for colour and seems to know what will sell. She always wears clothes from stock to show them off and persuades Katrina to do the same. Although Sue and Katrina often go out to meals together their social lives are kept quite separate. Sue has a penchant for wild parties and disco's whereas Katrina prefers quiet dinner parties and trips to the theatre.

CHARLES HARRIS

A tall well built fifty year old, who works as a bodyguard and spends a lot of time out of the country. He lives next door to Katrina's new house, and when he sees her moving in he is immediately attracted to her. However, in spite of taking her out several times he tries to keep the relationship platonic, because he knows that his job usually causes problems. He is often called away unexpectedly, ruining dinner parties and trips to the theatre and he doesn't feel he can make a commitment.

There is also the problem of Sonja, his first wife. She is slightly unstable mentally and although they have been divorced for some time she still likes him to take her out and look after her from time to time.

He is a man who loves his job and is beginning to worry that his days in the field are coming to an end, and the dreaded desk job is rearing its ugly head. When he is injured on a job, it seems like the end of the world to him. Only his great love for Katrina keeps him going.

SONJA HARRIS

Charles' ex-wife. A fashion plate of a woman, who designs and sells clothes to the rich and powerful. Likes her own way at all times and enjoys manipulating people. Hates Charles to have anything to do with other women, and plots to get rid of them from his life as soon as she can. Very bitchy to Katrina every time they meet. Has always been very rich and thinks that money can buy anything.

ABOUT THE AUTHOR

In 1977 after a busy life of nursing (she trained at The Royal London Hospital) extensive travelling, marriage to a busy GP bringing up two children and later helping with the grandchildren, Janet Cameron Simm and her second husband, a retired lecturer, moved to Somerset. At last she had the time to fulfil a long held ambition to write her first novel. Being a late starter in this field she found she had the experience to draw on that hopefully makes her writing more true to life. Having thoroughly enjoyed writing her first novel she is now busy writing her second.